Ink Vine and Other Swamp Stories

Elizabeth Broadbent

"A Mouthful of Roses" by Elizabeth Broadbent. Copyright © 2023. First published in *Ghostlight, The Magazine of Terror*, Great Lakes Association of Horror Writers. Reprinted with permission of the author.

"Questions a Man Ought Not to Ask" by Elizabeth Broadbent. Copyright © 2023. First published in *The Black Beacon Book of Horror* edited by Cameron Trost. Black Beacon Books. Reprinted with permission of the author.

"A Living Pentecost" by Elizabeth Broadbent. Copyright © 2024. First published in *If There's Anyone Left, Volume 4*, edited by Jason P. Burnham, C.M. Fields, and Wen Wen Yang, If There's Anyone Left. Reprinted with permission of the author.

"Babylon Burning" by Elizabeth Broadbent. Copyright © 2024. First published in *Judicial Homicides: Tales of Executions*, edited by D.L. Winchester. Undertaker Books. Reprinted with permission of the author.

"Folded in Light" by Elizabeth Broadbent. Copyright © 2023. First published in *Haven Speculative*, December 2023. Reprinted with permission of the author.

Ink Vine by Elizabeth Broadbent. Copyright © 2024. First published as *Ink Vine*. Undertaker Books. Reprinted with permission of the author.

"To Sing is to See," "For Thine is the Kingdom," and "Swamp Girl" Copyright © 2026 by Elizabeth Broadbent

All rights reserved.

No part of this publication may be reproduced, distributed, or transmitted in any form or by any means, including photocopying, recording, or other electronic or mechanical methods, without the prior written permission of the publisher, except as permitted by U.S. copyright law. For permission requests, contact Undertaker Books.

The story, all names, characters, and incidents portrayed in this production are fictitious. No identification with actual persons (living or deceased), places, buildings, and products is intended or should be inferred.

No generative Artificial Intelligence was used to create the text or cover art of this publication, nor its promotional materials. Undertaker Books logo designed by Cyan LeBlanc.

Cover Designer: Drew Huff

Anniversary edition 2026

Contents

Foreword	vii
A Mouthful of Roses	1
To Sing is to See	10
Some Fall	13
Questions a Man Ought Not to Ask	21
Babylon Burning	37
For Thine Is the Kingdom	50
A Living Pentecost	57
Folded in Light	60
Ink Vine	68
Swamp Girl	163
Acknowledgments	169
About the Author	173
Thank You from Undertaker Books	175
UB Website	177

Praise for Elizabeth Broadbent and Ink Vine

"Broadbent's world lures you in with gentle tendrils of growth and fragrant flowers and only when you are in its viney grasp do you realize you are trapped in its thrall as the swamp burbles up its ghastly tales."

— Kate Maruyama, author of *Alterations*, *The Collective*, and *Bleak Houses*

"With lyrical prose and haunting imagery that will chill you to your bones, Broadbent's new collection weaves hypnotic tales of home and heartache, of family secrets and small town angst, where echoes of the past swirl seductively within the sinister clutches of the swamp itself, where all things here take root. *Ink Vine & Other Swamp Stories* is an excellent display of Southern gothic at its finest."

— Candace Nola, author of *Shadow Manor*

"A stunning debut with a narrative voice so strong, you'll feel the swamp breathing down your neck. Eerie and very moving."

— Tim McGregor, author of *Eynhallow* and *Wasps in the Ice Cream*

"*Ink Vine* is a lush and deliciously queer Southern Gothic romance about desire and the things we will do to sate it. Broadbent's richly drawn characters and smart, evocative prose gives new meaning to the phrase 'blossoming love.' Emerald's longing--for acceptance, for love, for something more--haunts every word and sets the stage for a beautiful narrative about acceptance, self-discovery, and the power of connection."

— Jolie Toomajan, editor of *Aseptic and Faintly Sadistic*

"Elizabeth Broadbent combines a steamy love story with important observations about desperation, fear, and acceptance. *Ink Vine*, with its elements of dark fantasy and botanical horror, reminded me of *True Blood!*"

— Christi Nogle, author of the Bram Stoker Award winning first novel *Beulah*

"Broadbent writes the South as it is lived: lush, cruel, and impossible to escape. Her prose is lyrical and cutting, dismantling myth and silence alike. These stories are bruising, beautiful, and truly unforgettable."

— Aimee Hardy, author of *Pocket Full of Teeth*

Foreword

I wrote my first speculative fiction story in 2022. Several months before, my decade-long journalism career imploded when Scary Mommy was purchased by BDG, a media outlet owned by a man famed for both gutting Gawker.com and buying Napoleon's hat. When I say I wrote for Scary Mommy, smiles often turn condescending. *Mommy blogger*, people think. But before its sale, Scary Mommy boasted a staff of about a dozen and scored millions of hits per month. We wrote about the intersections of feminism, liberal politics, mental health, and parenting, giving voice to unseen women in the trenches of motherhood. We also carved out a space for vital political commentary that those busy and often-ignored women actually read. If you found yourself chasing small children between 2014 and 2022, you read my essays, or if you haunted social media during those years, you likely read them, too.

During that time, I also appeared on CNN, MSNBC, NPR's *All Things Considered*, and Canadian National Public Radio (BBC World News happened a bit later). I wrote essays for, among other places, *The Washington Post, Time*, and *Insider*. But AI's insidious rot had already begun, and venues were cutting jour-

Foreword

nalism gigs. By the summer 2022, my career had winnowed to a single venue, *ADDitude Magazine*. And while *ADDitude*, the first print publication for people with ADHD, remains a vital voice for neurodivergent rights, you can't cobble a career from one outlet.

That summer afternoon, I was writing to an audience of exactly no one. To say I was grief stricken and demoralized is an understatement.

I was on vacation then, sitting in a beach house in Nag's Head, North Carolina. We had recently relocated from South Carolina to Richmond, a move that tore me in two. I wanted to live closer to family; I wanted to snatch my sons away from the home state's dangerous right-wing politics—Dylann Roof bought his ammunition two miles from my old house. But I had left my friends behind. I had left the land. I knew its plants, its geology, its natural history. I knew its fossil beds. I knew the gossip, and I knew the stories. James Louis Petigru's nineteenth adage stands: South Carolina remains too small to be a republic, too large to be an insane asylum. Since I graduated from the honors college at the state's flagship university, everyone who does anything in South Carolina is probably a friend of a friend. When I moved four hundred miles away, I lost my orientations and my anchors. The maps were gone; the compasses spun. Who do we become when we no longer know the stories?

So when I opened my laptop that day, I didn't set my work in Virginia. I set it at home, in South Carolina swamp country, in the mud that made me who I am, where one day my ashes will scatter among alligators and green herons and old grandfather cypresses. I didn't take notes. I wrote; the narrative unfurled like a tapestry—the graduate student come to a small town, the witch both annoyed and intrigued, a back story about her mother and a hurricane and a sheriff who hates her guts. I gave it a very long title, "Questions a Man Ought Not to Ask," and sent it off.

Lower Congaree started there: with grief, with loneliness, with a fierce love for home, and that's swamp witch Talitha Merle. Readers have seen her in *Ink Vine* and *Ninety-Eight Sabers*. Talitha has her own novel, too. It's a heartbreak of a book, and it'll come in its own good time.

I could gin up very academic lies about Lower Congaree's persistence. I could tell you how Southern Gothic characters exist not as themselves, but as webs of interconnected relationships. How their use over multiple works is a function of Southern culture, Southern stories, and Southern history. How their layered constructions allow Southern Gothic authors to examine a broad sweep of society and historical events in ways that a single story can't. How this method highlights the characters' complex relationship with history both writ large and personal in a genre obsessed with submerged and suppressed narrative. I could cite example after example of reused settings and characters across multiple works in practice, from the obvious Faulkner (Yoknapatawpha) to Randall Kenan (Tim's Creek) to Jesmyn Ward (Bois Sauvage) to my own teacher, South Carolina's George Singleton (Forty-Five, Gruel, and Calloustown). I could, in fact, write an essay about why Southern Gothic authors do this (see "The H-Word," *Nightmare Magazine*, February 2026).

I'd like to pretend I sat down and had cogent academic arguments with myself. But I was homesick. Stories spread outward, billowing like smoke unfurled from a central soul of flame. The reason for Lower Congaree, in the beginning, was simple. I missed South Carolina.

And yes, South Carolina remains a banana republic with a marginally functional postal service. Institutional racism, corruption, and type 2 diabetes have replaced institutional racism, corruption, and pellagra. I once swam in radioactive water after an undisclosed uranium leak from a nuclear plant; when we left Columbia, the tap water tasted like moss. South Carolina is a state where the Murdaugh family ran Hampton County like their personal feudal estate for a century, and ran it so brutally that Wal-Mart refused to move in for fear of a lawsuit. People say that in the 1980s, one man wrote the state budget in a weekend while the rest of the legislature partied. I could tell you story after story of corruption and insanity, from a college boyfriend's assignations with a lieutenant governor to a US senator cheating at pool, down to the everyday misery of prejudice and racism that makes daily living a hell. The Deep South is as awful as it sounds.

And yet, this morning, I woke wet eyed from a dream: I stood in my old house. My husband hadn't told us that we'd left half our things behind—items I didn't remember, possessions I didn't know I owned. We were leaving again.

I love and hate South Carolina in equal measure. If I could write an essay about South Gothic character and setting, I could write a book on Southern Gothic authors' ambivalence toward our native land, using myself as a case study.

Love it or hate it, one story led to another like beads on a string. Once you start, it's hard to stop. This person is related to this person, who did this because this person did that. Like Thomas Wolfe said in *Look Homeward, Angel*, "Each of us is all the sums he has not counted: subtract us into the nakedness and night again, and you shall see begin in Crete four thousand years ago the love that ended yesterday in Texas." So I wrote and I kept writing, and the stories kept fitting together, because I know these people in Lower Congaree, and I know what they'd do.

I know who their mama is and what she'd do, too. I know what their neighbors would say about it. I know what abandoned house they stopped and wondered at; I know the route their bus took to school. I know the kindly town doctor who stitched their busted head, then went home and drank. He hit his son. The Marine recruitment center never closes but the nail salons come and go. The mechanic's name is Blake and he sends his boy Pat-Pat to tow cars when they tip into ditches. And woven through Lower Congaree, forming and shaping it, is the swamp.

The swamp—maybe that's the other beginning. We used to drive out there in college, before it was a national park, and always at night. Congaree Swamp is a haunted place. I said it right in *Blood Cypress* (Raw Dog Screaming, 2025):

Stand on the edge of that swamp, right where water and land become uncertain brothers, and that soupy air turns scum-sweet. Gaze back into those cypresses that seem old as bones. The distance goes gray and dim even when the sun shines. There'll be cicadas shrieking and mosquitoes buzzing, but under it all you'll hear the quiet. You'll feel it then. The hair on your neck will rise, and you'll know it's watching. You'll know it's waiting, too, and if you step wrong it'll suck you down into that muck with every other lost thing. It was there before us, and it'll be there after. That's the real reason they never cut that swampland.

To understand Lower Congaree, you have to understand that.

Welcome to swamp country.

Thank you to my readers. We write in hope of connection, but stories are a message in a bottle, words flung into the waves. We live with no certainty of their landing.

Here, stranger. These are for you.

INK VINE
AND OTHER SWAMP STORIES

ELIZABETH BROADBENT

A Mouthful of Roses

After the injury, when Heyward saw his heart beat to life in a doctor's bloody hands, his mother said warm air would do him good. A wildly outdated idea—Iraq had been hot enough—but she kept hinting about her aunt Alda. Great-aunt Alda, who lived in South Carolina with her mother's pearls, her husband's pension, and a house slowly sinking into the swamp. He could have handed his mother several decent arguments, but that would have been rude, so Heyward let her stuff him onto a southbound sleeper with two suitcases and a gift bag of Virginia peanuts.

Aunt Alda lived in Lower Congaree, down a long drive bushwhacked from a swamp-forest desperate to choke it. That swamp's darkness seemed a blind, swallowing thing. As his aunt led him inside, the smell of decay stuck thick in the Carolina humidity. Heyward spent a restless night on lace sheets, and in the morning, his aunt gave him a dining-room breakfast of biscuits and bacon, grits and eggs. Heyward chugged black coffee and ate like a man starved.

"—thought you might like to see the Lanier twins today," she was saying.

"Ma'am?" he asked.

"I said I thought you might like to visit the Lanier twins today rather than sit around with an old lady. It's good for young people to see other young people. They're pretty things, identical. A little strange but—they're a bit younger than you, just eighteen. They hardly see anyone, parents always abroad and they're cooped up in that big house."

Heyward mumbled something that could have been interpreted as "yes ma'am" or "no ma'am" depending upon the listener's inclination.

"Good!" His aunt clapped her pale, veiny hands. She was probably trying to fix him up, likely with his mother's blessing—probably the real reason they'd trundled him down to this swamp in the first place. Aunt Alda could have waited til he unpacked.

The Lanier house would have been called a mansion if the word wasn't rude. Its tall columns shone; rockers graced its long, white porch. Pink azaleas rioted in a quiet sort of way, and live oaks dripped theatrical Spanish moss. But red roses threaded through a fence that held back cypress trees, and the fetid scent of standing water rose beyond. Insects shrieked. The grounds seemed carved from a swamp determined to devour them.

His aunt had never told him the girls' names. Heyward's footfalls seemed too loud as he climbed the porch steps, and that swamp-scent grew sharper. Something could be watching from behind those cypresses; they crowded close and anything could be hiding in that greenish gloom, anything at all. As he lifted his hand to ring the bell, the door opened.

The girl had blue eyes, blonde hair, and features sharp as a fox's. She was barefoot, and her pale pink toes matched her pale pink fingernails. "You must be Heyward Trenholm Jones," she said, tilting her head as she examined him. Two beats passed, three. Should he say something? Was she waiting for him to speak? His heart kicked up, then she said, "Well, you might as well come in," and stepped aside. "I'm Esme." Her white dress was scandalously short, and what girl wore a dress at home on a Tuesday afternoon, anyway? "My sister's through here."

"It's nice to meet you," Heyward replied as they threaded through rooms of polished wood and silk upholstery. The cool, dim house seemed stuck in antebellum splendor; red roses graced nearly every table. Their rich smell, a step from sweet-rot, hung through the house.

"Your aunt told us you're twenty and your mother's a Trenholm," Esme said. "And you're from Richmond and you just got out of the army."

Heyward ruffled his overgrown crewcut. "Yeah—yes."

"Heroic of you. We thought it was funny. No one joins the army anymore."

"Someone has to do it," he replied stiffly.

"Yes, but it's usually other someones." Esme turned a corner, and the wood gave way to plush pinks. An identical girl in an identical dress sat on a silk couch, legs tucked almost lady-like at her side. A glass of sweet tea sweated beside another vase of roses. "Oh," she said, turning from a muted TV, where swans glided across a pond. "So this is him."

"Heyward, this is Imogen," Esme told him, and Heyward almost groaned at her scripted Southern politeness. "Imogen, this is Heyward."

"It's nice to meet you," Heyward replied.

"Pleasure, I'm sure." Imogen looked back at the swans.

"We should offer you a drink and amuse you now," Esme said. "What would you like to drink and how would you like to be amused?"

He managed not to cringe. "Please don't put yourselves out."

"I know what we should drink." Esme smirked at Imogen, then opened the liquor cabinet.

"Some water would be fine, and if you'd tell me where—" Heyward began.

"Pappy O'Daniel." Esme held out a dark bottle.

Heyward focused on his Sperrys. "Oh no, please, it's early yet for me, and we shouldn't—"

Imogen took the bottle and swigged it like milk. "I heard Trenholm boys could always drink."

What could he do but chug a shot? It burned going down. He passed the bottle to Esme, and her sister tugged him onto the couch. Silently, they watched swans and drank. "May I use your restroom?" Heyward asked when he couldn't wait any longer.

Esme waved a hand behind her. "First door on the left."

It was the third, and when he came back, whispers rose from the quiet room. He pulled back to listen. "At least he should pass out soon," Esme said. "Then we won't have to bother with him anymore."

"What if he doesn't?" Imogen asked.

"We'll figure something out."

"He's adorable, though. Wish there were two of him."

They giggled until Esme spoke again. "Wonder if he was wounded."

"Maybe. He's young to get sent home."

"If he was wounded, maybe . . ."

"We couldn't get that lucky."

They didn't want him there. He ought to leave, but he'd drunk too much to drive, and what did they mean about him being wounded? Heyward could have asked but eavesdropping was unpardonable, so he walked, rather unsteadily, back to the couch. Imogen passed him the bottle again. "We should go swimming now," she announced when they'd finished the bourbon.

Heyward's throat tightened as if he'd swallowed a hard marble. They would see his scar. "I'm sorry," he said. "I don't have a suit."

"You can borrow a suit." Imogen stood. When Esme got up,

they became indistinguishable: blondly beautiful, doe eyed and long limbed. His army buddies would have committed war crimes for them, or perhaps over them.

"I'll get you one of Daddy's suits," said one.

"We'll change. Then you can change in the pool house."

"I'd really rather not swim," Heyward managed.

"We want you to swim with us. You wait here and we'll be right down." They disappeared. What could he do? When women requested something, he did it or risked barbarity. Heyward ground his teeth and jiggled his leg as paired swans drifted, unbothered, until the twins appeared in matching scarlet bikinis. He tried not to look at their high breasts and flat stomachs.

"Here." One girl thrust a pair of trunks at him. "Go change in the pool house."

He had to try. "I'd prefer not to, if you don't mind."

"But we always swim now." The twin flipped her hair over her shoulder.

There was no helping it. Heyward stood. The army had taught him to drink, but they'd always swilled bottom-shelf liquor. This expensive stuff made him dizzy. How were those slim girls still standing?

Reeling, Heyward trailed the twins through that maze of antique glory. Outside, crepe myrtle and subtropical shrubbery surrounded their saltwater pool; red roses grew thick around its fence and their scent nearly covered the rotten smell of standing water. Something about that swamp—it seemed to be watching, always watching. But it was only a swamp, and he was drunk.

The girls pointed Heyward to a changing room with silver hooks, fluffy towels, and an inexplicable armchair. He stripped and pulled on the trunks, which fit closely and high on the thigh. At least that time in the hospital hadn't wasted his military muscle. He had that, if nothing else. The scar was ugly but they couldn't call him skinny.

The girls stared when he walked squinting into the white Carolina sun. Heyward braced for their questions.

"What happened to your *chest*?" one twin almost demanded.

Heyward tried to look heroic but winced instead. "I was wounded."

"But what *happened*?"

"A roadside bomb."

The other girl stepped up to him. Delicately, almost thoughtfully, she traced the jagged pucker on his chest. Plum-purple, it zig-zagged sharply to his left. Heyward stilled. A girl had never touched him like that. Somehow, he stopped himself from teetering. "But how, though?" she asked.

"A bomb went off, just outside base. Shrapnel hit my chest." He blushed. "But they got me to triage, cracked my chest, and massaged my heart. I came back." He kept it as simple as possible. He didn't say that his eyes had opened to see hands on his own raw-red heart, or that no one should feel his rib cage gaped wide.

The twins exchanged a look. "What d'you mean, you 'came back'?" one asked.

Heyward blushed harder. "I died."

"You died?" The other narrowed her eyes. "You mean your heart stopped? Completely?"

He nodded.

"Huh." The twins exchanged an oddly conspiratorial glance. "Let's swim, then."

Esme and Imogen tanned on floats and whispered to one another. Heyward's attempts at conversation drew one-word answers. The sun beat high and hard and his mouth dried.

"We need drinks," said a twin. She got out and strode inside.

"The swamp seems too close," he told the other.

"It's always close," she said.

Her sister returned juggling two pitchers and three stacked glasses. "Sweet tea for us and lemonade for you. Here." She shoved a glass at Heyward, who chugged it, then lifted himself from the pool and poured another.

The twins sipped in silence.

"We should go inside," one said eventually.

"Yeah, let's," replied the other.

Heyward tried to climb out, but found it much harder than before; he scrabbled and nearly fell. Hot sun could be hell on a drunk. A twin smiled wickedly. "I want to dry you off, army boy," she said, picking up a towel.

Heyward's pulse quickened. Imogen, who'd said he was cute?

"No, *I* want to dry him off." The other grabbed a towel, too.

The first twin blinked sweetly. "We can share. We're good at sharing." Both girls began rubbing him down, more caressing than drying. What was happening? Heyward focused on the swamp twining just beyond the pool rather than their hands. Again he felt like something was watching. He snapped back when a girl trailed her fingers over his scar. "Did you see anything?"

"What do you mean?" he asked.

"When you died."

Heyward shook his head and nearly toppled as he world spun. He always shook his head, though he'd seen white light.

"We should show you something," said one twin.

"You won't believe it," the other told him. She grabbed his hand with her small, soft one.

"Can I change first?" he asked, blinking hard.

They gave each other that shared look which seemed to mean something significant. "No," said the one holding his hand. "It won't take long and anyway"—she smiled—"we like looking at you."

They marched him back through the cool house that smelled of roses. Heyward couldn't have walked a straight line. "I can't say the alphabet backward," he said for no real reason.

"Of course you can't," replied a twin. "No one can."

"Look," said one. When they stopped in a formal dining room, he almost fell. "See that table?"

The mahogany behemoth looked like all the others. "What about it?"

"This house was a hospital during the War. But all the men were gone and our however- many-greats-grandmother, she did surgeries right there on that table."

"She had to find a bonesaw." The other twin played with his hand. "But she used the family's silver knives. We still carve turkeys with them."

Her sister pursed her lips. "I think the table's big enough."

"For what?"

The girl petting with his hand smirked. "*You* know what."

They were making fun of him. This didn't happen in real life. "Y'all, any guy would love it. Really. But I didn't come over so you could laugh at me."

"We're not laughing. You should get on the table."

"Esme's serious." Imogen, it was Imogen holding his hand, and she whispered in his ear. "If you get on the table I'll kiss you. We never have boys over."

Somehow, Heyward scrambled up. Esme giggled and pushed him onto his back.

He laughed. His head lay at one end of the table, his feet at the other. Their shoving made him dizzy again, and he laughed some more.

One twin leaned on either side. "So," said a girl, "have you ever kissed anyone?"

"No." Heyward didn't blush. He'd kiss them. He'd kiss either of them, both of them. The wood was almost cold on his back, and the ceiling so white, like something he couldn't quite recall.

"We're much smaller than you, so this wouldn't be fair otherwise," one was saying as she drew his hands together over his head. A rope tightened on them.

"Hey now," he managed, because he ought to. But the rope made it better.

The other traced his scar. "It's almost pretty," she said, then kissed it.

Heyward's vision blackened at the edges. "I am very drunk," he tried to say.

"What was that? I couldn't understand. You drank too much lemonade." A girl giggled far away.

"Shhhh. You should be quiet." Something soft touched his lips, then slipped inside. Another silky red sliver slid into his mouth, then another. Clumsily, Heyward moved his tongue around them. Flowers. They were stuffing his mouth with roses. He could hardly move. His eyelids felt so heavy and they were so beautiful.

"A virgin and a dead man." More giggling. "So sad he got drunk and wandered into the swamp."

"It'll like him."

"It'll *love* him."

"He looks so pretty like this. It's almost sad to do it."

"But it'll give us whatever we want for a twice-dead virgin."

"You do it, though."

What did they mean? Heyward couldn't string words together. This had something to do with whatever those roses held back. There was rot beyond them, an old rot twisted deep in that swamp, something that watched and waited and wanted. Silver flashed. The ceiling was white, white. Heyward tried to scream when blue eyes met his. Instead his tongue twisted in roses.

To Sing is to See

At dusk a dark cloud exploded from the chimney. It became a maelstrom of beating black wings, each spinning off until there was none at all. I cursed, because if birds in a house were good luck, bats in a house were the worst, but I wanted to stay alone in the woods and finish writing that novel. This one-room shack rented cheap; it was mostly inaccessible and at least the chimney was sealed at the bottom.

My mother always said, "Meadow, you're not afraid of a little flying mouse, are you?"

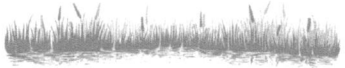

AFTER A MONTH AND A HALF, the bats and I had a routine. I woke in the single room to their chittering. I wrote all day against a background of their squeaks. They seemed to be fussing as they jostled for space, or maybe trilling in jubilation when they unearthed a juicy bug. At night, if I listened hard, I could almost pick out a cadence and grammar, nouns and verbs, names and places. They seemed so close, a heartbeat away.

Sometimes I stopped writing and listened harder.

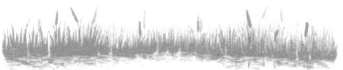

ONCE A BABY BAT WAS BORN, and it clung tight to a wall while its mother dipped and dived for insects. She sang while it nursed, because to sing is to see, and the baby knew that when she grew, she would pass through darkness on silent wings and shape song into pictures.

I stopped writing my novel. At least I only wasted two and a half months before I knew it was trash. I wrote their stories instead.

A bat bragged that once she had grabbed a moth so big and fat it wouldn't fit in her mouth. It had been slow and sluggish, a low flier, and antennae had tickled her throat as she tore its wings. They laughed her down with sneering squeaks. But I knew.

She had killed a luna moth.

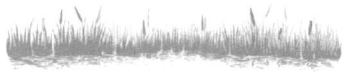

I WAS EARTHBOUND AND DARKBLIND. They spoke of flying at night, of sound singing against leaves or rock or soft-winged owls. From five fingers, bats created flight. My hands were clever for writing books or cooking food. But my limbs did not lift me. I could learn the bitter crunch of beetles and moths but never a bat's true joy.

They consoled me with gentle chirps and cheeps. But they

alone could rise on dark-beating wings. I stayed muddy and clumsy. If I closed my eyes I slammed into walls, walls I couldn't climb with clever claws.

THAT SECRET WAS LONG FORGOTTEN, the bats tweeted, but I had learned their stories. I could be worthy, if I managed it. I could become like them. Is that all it takes? I asked. Yes, they trilled, yes, yes, it's so simple. You must see in song, because to sing is to see. My knife twisted. When I screamed, they scattered, a flurry of frantic chitters. Blood-slippery, I twisted the knife again. Wings beat a whirlwind in my new darkness.

Some Fall

I smelled that hurricane sure as if I'd seen its yellow sky. Lee only laughed.

"They say it'll hit the coast at the North Carolina border and go up to the Outer Banks, baby doll." He kissed my nose. "It ain't coming nowhere near Lower Congaree."

They say, they say. Men'll believe the weatherman who says it's sunny while rain falls on their heads. Crows flapped restlessly in their roost. My daughter lay quiet in my belly, and the tree frogs lost their voices. That smell strengthened, sharper than ozone, sticky like salt-spray. I slept while I could. When I woke, dawn was breaking red over the tupelo trees, and our baby was coming. Outside, I found Lee squinting at low-slung anvil clouds.

"It's time," I told him. "Before you ask, no herbs or anything . . ." I stopped; we didn't use words for what I did. "I can't stop it."

"That hurricane slammed Charleston last night," he said. "It's headed straight upstate. They say it's the strongest we ever seen." His blond hair ruffled when the wind kicked up. "Jane, I shoulda listened. We need to—"

"Did you hear me?" I could have shaken him, but I touched his cheek instead.

"Are you sure the baby's—"

Deep in my belly, something tightened. I forced myself to chart its force and tension, power and pressure. "Was I right about that hurricane?"

"Yes, but—"

"Then nail plywood over the windows. Move the car into the field, away from the trees." I pressed my lower back. "Imma walk this baby out."

A few women in Lower Congaree birthed their babies at the hospital in Columbia. Most sent for me, like they'd sent for my mother before. I knew how to call a child to the waking world. But I also remembered those words my mother had whispered to me before every labor: *Stay strong, Jane. Every birthing woman walks a knife's edge. Some fall.*

Lee dragged plywood from the barn while I paced to his hammer's rhythm. Wind shuddered the swamp oaks; leaves' silvered backs rose like hackles. With a first baby, I should have lasted a day after those early contractions. Instead, each gripped harder, deeper. Their slight tightness bloomed to a regular cramping that wrapped around my belly and settled brutally in my lower back. Labor usually gives a mercy of rest between contractions, but my pain became an unending misery. I'd sweet-talked plenty of women through back labor, but that wraparound pain worried me. If my daughter faced forward, she'd have to flip. If she didn't, I'd labor long, and I'd labor hard.

You just keep walking, sweetie, I'd say to women. *Keep it up, honey. You're doing so well.* Lord, I'd pour that sugar on thick. Or I'd outright lie: *You'll have that baby in no time. He's coming soon, don't you worry.* I'd even try to distract them—*Do you have names picked out? Do you think it'll be a boy or a girl?* Some were smart enough to throw that question right back. *You tell me, Jane,* they'd say.

I would, too. I always knew. I could cradle their bellies and tell them, *You're having a boy.* As they lit up, I'd tell their sons, *It's time.*

It was too early to clench my teeth, but I was clenching them as my bare feet slid on fallen leaves and prickled on pinestraw. I'd want something to bite before long. It shouldn't have hurt so bad so soon.

It's time for you now, baby girl, I told her. *It's time, and you're coming fast.*

But she wasn't shoving and eager to see the waking world; my own body was desperate to push her out. I could cool a fever or call down rain, but I couldn't slow my own labor.

"Jane!" When Lee grabbed my arm, I startled hard. "Jane, honey, the rain's starting. You gotta get inside."

"I have to walk," I said. "There's nowhere to walk in that house."

"You can't walk in the rain." He picked up my hand. I yanked it back to press my hip. When Lee placed his palms over mine and steered me in, I sighed at that sweet weight.

I paced circles in the kitchen—back and forth, back and forth, like a pig in a pen. Rain rat-a-tat-tatted harder and faster; wind shrieked into furious gusts. Lee walked behind me, his weight pressed into my hips.

"Harder," I said.

"Harder and I'll leave bruises, honey." His thumbs dug into my back.

"Doesn't matter." I sucked a quick gasp as pain spiraled. My daughter's panic peaked, a trapped bird battering walls, windows. *Shhh,* I said. *It's hard to come into the world.* "Boil water," I told my husband. "Use the woodstove, 'cause the power's 'bout to die."

"I'll have to let go of you."

"It needs done." I bit back a moan as his hands left me. I wanted that pressure on my hips and I wanted Lee's hands on me. "Why am I boiling water?" he asked.

"I need something sterile to cut the cord." I didn't tell him that I might need to cut myself. *Better to nip a bit of room and ease the way,* my mother always told me. *If the baby's head won't come, cut a titch. Don't let a woman tear.* I didn't worry about using a knife on myself. Amid this misery, I wouldn't feel it.

I should've watched a clock. I should've calculated: *Each contraction lasts this long, and they are this far apart.* Instead I told time by that hurricane. I knew I'd labored long when its rain became a torrent and my pain soared into agony.

Lee couldn't stop that hurt, but he held me through it. Mama called it the true test of a man; most ran from labor's blood and pain. A very few stayed. *The ones who love their wives the most won't let them suffer alone,* she'd say.

"Should you sit? Should you walk?" Lee asked as I groaned. "You need to drink."

I needed to drink. I had to drink. He'd filled the tub before the power went. When had the power gone? When had he lit the candles? Lee handed me a glass of water. I sipped, then stumbled to the sink and threw up. That was victory: I hadn't vomited on the hardwoods. *Hold on, baby girl,* I said. *We're gonna do this, you and me.*

But she'd gone still as a fawn in the forest, and my words wouldn't reach her.

I'd seen women scream. I'd seen women pray for death. I'd sworn to birth my daughter in dignified silence. When you gave yourself freedom to feel it, pain lost its power. I knew that secret. But my pain never ended, and I couldn't breathe through it because it didn't stop. Wind stole my moans; as its strength grew, they disappeared in it. My torment rose with the rain. Trees bent and groaned with me. Lee rubbed my back.

"Keep walking baby," he told me. "Keep going."

"Oh God, it hurts," I said. "It's not supposed to hurt like this."

"Keep walking," he repeated.

I screamed. I clenched my fists so hard that my nails tore my palms. When those contractions soared into the unimaginable, when I wondered how a person could hurt so bad and not die, I was ready. Lee wrapped around me while I squatted and pushed hard. Nothing happened. It would take time. He gave me water and throw-up splashed my bare legs. I pushed and screamed through every cruel contraction. My husband held me up.

The hurricane lashed us. His mouth moved; wind stole his voice. The world had narrowed to a white-hot point of pain. "It's been an hour," he shouted.

An hour. I shouldn't have had to push for so long but it didn't matter, because I could do nothing but keep pushing. Sweat stung my eyes. The house whined in the wind, like it wanted to fly apart at the seams. I lay down. I crouched; I bent on all fours. Lee held me up, pressed my back, wrapped around me. Every time that pain spiraled up, up, up, I pushed.

Lee yelled. He yelled again. I caught "three hours."

It was going on too long. I breathed deep and tried to float atop that fear.

My daughter wasn't moving, and how much longer could I push? It didn't matter. I would push until she came.

As I tried again, sweat-slippery, shaky, mid-contraction, something inside me seemed to slip. Water rushed down my thighs. Lee's eyes blew huge and why was he making that face over amniotic fluid? But my water had broken hours ago—blood pooled on the floor. That cruel pain faded. My daughter slid backward, and I dropped to my knees. The world went fuzzy.

"Jane?" Lee shouted. "Jane!"

No wind wailed and no rain lashed our roof. The eye was passing.

"Uterine rupture," I managed. He had to do it fast or we'd lose her. "Get a knife. I'll tell you how."

"No." Horror, fear, something else—his voice was cracking, too high. "I won't do it."

"Or else it'll be both of us. You have to do it now." I sank to the floor. *Some fall.*

Lee knelt beside me. "I can't."

"Now, or you'll lose her too!" I was going no matter what but my daughter did not have to follow. "Do it *now!*"

He set his jaw. "Take me. A life for a life. You can do it."

"Oh God, Lee, don't." The hardwoods were so cool. Good to sleep on. I pressed my cheek against them. No, I wouldn't sleep, and no, I wouldn't take Lee.

"I won't cut you open. Take me or the baby'll die." He grabbed my chin. I blinked hard. "Do you want her to die?"

"Don't you make me pick." I hated him. I loved him. I hated him.

"Do it. Her life for mine." Lee tucked a sweaty strand of hair behind my ear. "I love you, Jane. Do it now, before it's too late."

He wouldn't cut me. She'd die if I didn't. Goddamn him. No, I couldn't think that, not with what I was about to do.

"I love you," I told my husband. "We were happy, and I love you, Lee." I hated him so much. I could barely raise my arm, but I touched his forehead. Something seeped from him—a sweet power, a strength like I'd never known. I clutched it close. Lee yanked away, and the door slammed as he shambled out. In a sudden, smashing torrent, rain began one more time.

I slipped in my own blood, stood, and squatted. My daughter screamed into the wind as I caught her in my own two hands.

Dale Brewster and Preston Hewitt found us the next morning

when they busted down the door. I lay naked and bloody on the hardwoods with a baby at my breast. "Jesus fucking Christ," Dale finally said.

Preston only stared.

"Get the goddamn sheriff and an ambulance!" Dale shouted.

"Don't need an ambulance," I told him. "I need help getting to bed. Send Mary Joiner over here to—"

He knelt and picked up my hand. It must have taken a lot for Dale to kneel next to a naked, bloody woman. "That ambulance ain't for you, Jane," he said. "We found Lee in the yard. He's—" Dale sagged. "Lee passed on."

Knowing it was one thing and hearing it another. Tears took me. I did it to save our daughter's life, but I also saved my own, and how could I forgive myself for that?

I wept as Dale covered me in a blanket. "Did you name her?" he asked gently.

She had one name. She'd have two. "Ella Lee," I said through a sob. "She's Ella Lee, after her daddy."

The sheriff came, Lee's brother Lonny. His eyes narrowed as he scanned that kitchen: blood on the floor, vomit in the sink, my clothes scattered where I'd shed them. "What happened, Jane?" he asked.

"Lee went outside." It wasn't a lie.

"Why'd Lee go outside?"

"I don't know," I said, which wasn't a lie either.

"Jane." Lonny's gaze didn't drop. "There's a whole body's worth of blood on this floor. *Why did my baby brother go outside?*"

"He just did." I managed a whisper.

"Witch." He spoke too low for Dale and Preston to hear. "They might not know what happened. But I do."

"Lee picked." My voice was so small. "The baby and I were dying, and he picked."

"You killed him to save yourself." Lonny spit on the floor, then strode out. I cried again, and I cried because he was right. Lee had held me when I hurt most. I killed him anyway.

I hugged my daughter to my breast. Lee had died for me. But I'd killed for her.

There was nothing to do but keep living.

Questions a Man Ought Not to Ask

When he walked into Brewster's, old men in Vietnam vet ballcaps turned from their sausage and eggs. He took a seat at the counter and flipped his mug. Though we pretended to ignore him, we watched, and the diner at the back of the convenience store seemed too quiet as Shirley poured his coffee. "Whatchoo want?" she asked.

"The special," said the man. He wore ratty jeans and a thermal shirt, but his winter hat looked expensive, and his boots seemed made for hiking. Our men were hard muscled and rough palmed with hard work. He was slim and soft handed.

At least he didn't ask for cream and sugar.

I sipped my own bitter-black coffee from the other end of the counter.

Shirley dropped a plate of biscuits and gravy on his paper placemat. "You passing through?" she asked.

"I'm staying at the Gaston Motel," he replied. That was twenty miles and a world away, but the stranger didn't say it. He didn't have to. "I'm hoping to get to know some folks and hear some stories."

Shirley looked long, and looked hard. "We ain't got no stories in Lower Congaree."

He gave her a tiny smile. "I doubt that."

She ripped his scribbled bill from her pad and turned away.

Those students came up from the university every so often. "Tell me your local legends," they'd say, or, "I heard you believe in root medicine—do you have healers here?" They brought useless questions, questions a man ought not to ask. "Forget the biscuits," I called. "Just put the coffee on my tab."

Shirley didn't glance up. "Don't you worry 'bout it, Ella Lee."

I shivered down the street to a little house behind Hopkins General Store. Dixie's baby wanted to come too soon. "I'll bring you some things tomorrow," I told her, and laid my hands on her belly. He was thumb-sucking and opinionated already. I had to sweet-talk him. *Stay there for your mama. Just a little while longer, please?*

I gave Dixie that smile she wanted. "He'll stay put til I come again."

"He?" She grinned like spring had come early. Clint wanted a junior.

Outside, I hugged myself, fast-walking before my toes numbed despite my wool socks and old boots. I had to get back home—Dixie needed her things. Shirley's leg was hurting again. Mattie's back was acting up with this cold snap, and if I could manage something for Sue Ellen's migraines, she'd knit me some gloves. I never could knit. Mama always said I dropped stitches like the devil dropped cusses.

Anyway, my babies would be getting lonely.

I stepped around the puddle next to my truck, hopped into the driver's seat, and turned my key. The engine cranked and died.

Goddammit.

Someone knocked on the window. "Can I help you?" That damn student peered at me. He wasn't bad-looking with those dark eyes, that shoulder-length hair meant for pulling. They'd call him names over that hair. I liked it.

"Can you help me?" I asked. "I doubt it."

"It's either a dead battery or your starter. If you're unlucky, it's your alternator. Can I take a look?"

He might've worn fancy wool gloves, but he sounded like any man in Lower Congaree. I stepped out of the car. "Go ahead, city boy."

He stuck his head under her hood and poked around. "Your battery kicked the bucket. I can jump you, but it'll die again. Or I can take you to the hardware store, show you which to get, and put in the new one." He went quiet, like he'd said too much. "I mean, if you want."

Not a bad offer, and it would save me from paying Dale down at the garage. "Pick out the battery at the hardware store for me, then give my car a jump," I said. "If you follow me home and change it out, I'll make you something hot to eat." Then maybe something else. Maybe.

"I'm Henry Jenkins," he said.

"Ella Lee Merle. I'm halfway down Lost John Road—you'll have to follow me."

We went into Greene's Seed and Feed. Henry carried the battery and I let him do it, then played helpless while he jumped my Ford. Before he hooked up the positive clamp, he handed me those fancy gloves. I could've glared. I could've said I wasn't cold. My fingers were numb, and I pulled them on.

Our roads wove around the edges of blackwater swamp. They twisted like phone cords, and I didn't go slow. Henry kept on my tail, following those curves like he'd learned them long ago. "Fun ride," he said, popping out of his shiny Pontiac Firebird.

"You're a good driver." I had to hand him that.

He didn't seem to hear. Instead, he gazed at the bare-branched tupelo surrounding the swamp. My babies watched him. "You have a lot of crows up here."

"Mmm-hmm." They probably wondered who the hell he was, too.

Henry shivered, and in that fluffy new coat, he wasn't cold. "Crows always scared me."

"Why's that?"

"They're carrion eaters."

The lies they told about my babies. "Believe me, they'd rather not. If you change out that battery, I'll heat up some soup. That okay with you?"

He was already popping my hood. "Sounds great. I'll change your oil and poke around, check everything out for you, too."

I was good to him in that kitchen—vegetable soup, warm bread, sweet tea, and hot coffee. Lunch was finished just as he knocked. When I opened the door, Henry looked, then looked away. I should've expected it. Instead of a ratty winter coat, I wore soft jeans, a tight T-shirt, and a snuggly flannel that once belonged to my daddy. Henry hung his own coat. He had some muscle to his chest, and his arms weren't the sticks I'd imagined.

Lunch was small talk, stupid things. He liked my soup. He was a doctoral student working on his thesis, come from Carolina's anthropology department to collect folktales. No one had any luck in this area, and he thought he'd try. He'd grown up in Charlotte. His daddy was a mechanic, which explained why a soft-handed grad student could tell a dead battery from a faulty starter. "What d'you do?" he asked me when he finished.

"Oh, I stay over here and keep to myself," I told him.

"No boyfriend?" He smiled when he said it.

"Why?" I asked, sweet as my tea. "You auditioning?"

Henry had white, even teeth that someone had paid a lot of money for. "Maybe. You're too pretty to stay here all alone with those crows."

"You think so?" No one had called me pretty in a long time. The ones who had didn't have his long, dark hair, and while they might've fixed a roof tile or banged a loose chair together, they'd expected plenty of cooing over it.

"You're definitely too pretty to sit here in this swamp alone," Henry said.

I could've used any of those Joiner or McAllister boys, but they expected coddling, even from me. More than that, I'd come up with them. We'd climbed trees, lost teeth, and picked blackberries together; they belonged to Mattie or Sue Ellen or Dale. They belonged to Lower Congaree.

Henry didn't belong to us, and he couldn't stop looking.

"I like it here," I told him, then stood and walked toward my room. Thank the Lord Mama had taught me to make my bed every morning. "You coming?" I called.

Henry's chair scraped the floor. "Yes, ma'am."

I liked that boy already.

"THAT WAS UNEXPECTED." Henry sounded uncertain. We lay under my grandmother's quilt while I combed my fingers through his hair, shiny as a girl's.

"Mmmm." He didn't need answers.

"It was nice, don't get me wrong." He paused. "I mean, much more than nice. Just unexpected. God, my professors would kill me."

I cuddled closer. He was warm under my quilt, and it was good to be warm. That cold snap seeped into a person's bones. "Those stupid old men are a world away," I said. "Forget them."

His hand slipped down the small of my back. "I forgot to, um, ask. Exactly how old are you?" He chewed his lip like a little boy.

I tapped that pouty lip, like my mama once did to me. "Stop. You'll chap it. I'm old enough to buy liquor and not much more."

"That's young to be living all alone. I guess you got this place from your parents?"

"From my mama, when she died." My chest hurt.

"What about your father?"

I kissed his nose and said it fast so I never had to say it again. "My daddy died the day I was born, during a hurricane." Hurricane Denise was a big one, but it was supposed to make landfall at the North Carolina border. It turned, slammed Charleston, and tore straight up the state to Lower Congaree, like Mama had told my daddy it would. Her labor started as that storm hit. I near about killed her, and when daddy went out into the yard, the hurricane killed him." I didn't tell Henry that Mama had brought plenty of babies into the world, and she knew death was coming when she started to bleed out. Daddy had refused to watch her die. *Take me instead*, he'd said. *Save the baby.* He knew Mama could. In the morning, Dale and Preston Hewitt found him dead in the front yard. "My daddy's name was Lee Evans," I told Henry. "That's why I'm Ella Lee."

He pulled me closer. "You have your mother's last name, then."

"We do that in my family," I told him.

"Why?"

Men and their questions. "We just do. You as good a mechanic as you say?"

He shrugged, which meant yes.

"I'll talk to Dale tomorrow. He's looking for a man and if you want to fit into Lower Congaree, that's the best way to do it."

Henry pulled back a little. "You think so?"

I nodded. Then I kicked him out.

In the morning, we met at the diner, and everyone pretended not to watch as we sat together at the counter. "You pick up a straggler, Ella Lee?" Shirley asked when we turned our mugs.

I made a sound that could've meant yes and could've meant no.

She eyeballed Henry. "I guess you want the special again."

He nodded. "Yes, ma'am."

I knew better than to talk to Henry with everyone listening, and he was smart enough not to speak to me. But Shirley asked, "You want this check separate or together?"

"Together," Henry replied, damn him, which told everyone exactly how far we'd gone and exactly how he felt about it, too. They'd find out later that morning when I took him to the garage, but that news would've taken time to travel through town. By paying my bill, Henry guaranteed people would talk about nothing but that city boy grad student sleeping with Ella Lee.

As we walked out, the sheriff, my uncle Lonny Evans, fixed me with his meanest glare. I threw it right back. When Dale and Preston found my daddy, they'd called him.

"Why'd you have to go and do that?" I asked Henry as the store's cowbell clanged behind us. I resisted smacking him. They'd see from the window and talk about that, too.

"What?" Henry asked.

"Buy me breakfast."

"I thought it was the right thing to do?"

"You think that won't go all over town in a minute?"

Henry didn't look at me. "I guess it will."

"Did you think it would give you some sort of leg up?" I asked. "Use me like that again, and we'll run you out of town so fast your head'll spin."

That shut him up. As we trudged toward the garage, cold crept through my coat. "I didn't mean it that way," Henry said.

"Like hell you didn't."

I still took him to Dale, and I had to talk fast, but he said he'd try Henry for the day. Once he agreed, I smiled and gave him a small bag. "I know your hands get dry, working out here in this cold all day," I told him.

"That's sweet of you, Ella Lee," he said, and we had a deal.

With Henry settled, I hiked around Lower Congaree all morning, my hands going numb between houses. Dixie's baby had stayed settled—restless, she said, but settled. I visited Mattie, then Sue Ellen, who promised me a pair of gloves. Shirley was wiping down the counter when I showed my face at Brewster's again. "I have something for you," I told her.

She took the bag I handed her. "You brought that boy in this morning."

I made another sound that didn't mean anything.

"You sure you wanna mess around with that?" Her eyes were beady as a chicken's.

"You sure you wanna mess around in my business?"

She opened her mouth, then shut it.

"Uh-huh," I said. "That's right."

"How'd it go?" I asked Henry that night. Dark had already dropped, but he found my house without trouble.

"Dale said he'd hire me if I wanted a job." He started to sit.

I pointed toward the bathroom. "Not on my kitchen chair. You get in that shower first. I'll have dinner ready when you get out."

"You didn't have to make me dinner or have me over here again," he said. "I don't want you to feel—"

"I wanted to. And you wanted to come. So get your ass in that shower, then come eat some chicken." I didn't say, *This house gets lonely with only my babies for company. My bed'll be warm tonight, and it'll be good to wake up with someone in the morning.*

"That murder of crows was watching when I came in," he told me during dinner.

I made another one of those sounds. Later, I pulled his hair.

Henry kept working at the garage. He complained about paying the Gaston Motel for a room he wasn't using, and I told him to move everything to my place. "I don't want to impose," he said.

"It's not imposing," I told him.

He moved in.

I should've thought that out before I offered, 'cause then his questions started. I did most of my work while Henry was at the garage, but some tasks needed moonlight. "What were you doing last night, Ella Lee?" he asked one morning. "I woke up and you were gone. I thought maybe you were in the bathroom, but you didn't come back."

"I had things to do." I poured his coffee, then my own.

"What kind of things need done in the middle of the night?" He squinted at me.

I kissed his forehead. "Things you don't need to worry about."

Once in a while, Henry made some noise about those stories. "Worry about that later," I said. "You gotta get to know folks before they'll talk to you."

He passed me his cigarette—Henry had started bumming Dale's Pall Malls, then buying packs of his own. I drew my arms close as I dragged on it, and he tucked me under his arm. "If you'd let me smoke in the house—" he started.

"Nope." I took another puff. "No cigarettes in the house, and anyway, I like you hugging me."

Once, I found Henry tugging at my root cellar door. "What's this?" he asked.

"Herbs," I said. "I dry stuff in there." That seemed like

enough, especially when I kissed him. "Come inside. I need warmed up."

"God, those crows again. You have to find a way to keep them from roosting here," Henry said as he followed me back to the house. My babies glared from their tree. One flapped angrily.

"They live here, same as you, and don't say things like that, Henry Jenkins." I rubbed my hands together.

He shivered in his fluffy coat. "It's like they're judging me."

"They do when you say things like that." I pushed the door open and slipped inside, then poured myself a cup of coffee, partly to warm my fingers around the mug.

"Crows can't understand people," he said.

I sat in a kitchen chair my granddaddy had built for my grandmother. "Planning on leaving?"

He opened his mouth, shut it, and then finally managed, "I wasn't planning on it anytime soon, but if you want me to, I'll—"

"I didn't say I wanted you to. I'd rather you didn't. But if you're staying here, don't you talk bad about those crows." I got up to stir the stew. Henry played with his placemat.

He asked too many questions, but he didn't sit on his ass while I cleaned up. He helped. He brought me little presents from the general store—things I'd never buy myself, like cards or candy bars. He'd give me the last cigarette in his pack. I'd brought him home for a reason, but that's not why I kept him.

My mama had told me it happened like that with my daddy. "I made a plan to bring him here." She laughed. "Then I spun around and realized I was in love."

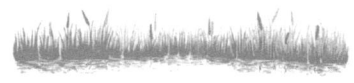

CLINT JUNIOR WAS a month old when Shirley told me to visit Dixie. "You need to git over there," she said as I turned my mug. "Dixie ain't well."

"She seemed fine when I ran into her at Hopkins yesterday," I told her.

Shirley glanced at Henry, then looked back at me. "You go see her."

Dixie had two black eyes, and I was gentle when I touched the bruise on her side. "He didn't break anything," I said. "This ain't the first time, is it?"

She stared across the room at a calendar, one that came free from Greene's Feed and Seed. "First time since the baby came. He said I have to stop nursing him."

I trudged out to my truck, then mucked back. Several days' worth of twelve-packs filled her supercan, assuming Clint stopped at twelve. "So he's done it before?" I asked when I came back with the salve I needed.

Dixie pressed her lips together and looked at that calendar again.

"Put this on three times a day. It'll help it heal and stop it from hurting," I told her. "How often does he do it?"

She must've known I wouldn't stop asking. "Maybe once or twice a week, but never where anyone can see. Do you have anything to dry me up?"

"I'll take care of it," I said as I straightened up. "Don't forget that salve."

"Thank you, Ella Lee," she told me. "God bless you."

Henry came home wide eyed that night, his lip chapped from chewing it. "I had to take the wrecker out to get Clint Booker's truck," he said. "He slammed it into a tupelo and went into the drainage ditch. The sheriff and the coroner were already there." He shuddered. "Ella Lee, I told you crows were carrion eaters. They took out his eyes. Why the hell he had his windows open in weather like this, I'll never know. Those crows were hanging around in the trees like they were waiting for more, too."

"Did you get the truck out okay?" I kissed his head.

"We did, but—"

"Good, 'cause his wife doesn't have another." I tapped Henry's lip. "Don't nibble like that. You chapped your lip up. Lemme get you something for that." I opened my extra pantry and rooted out some balm.

Henry smeared his lips and didn't speak til we sat down to dinner. "You have something for everything, don't you, Ella Lee?"

I tucked some of that pretty hair behind his ear. "Sometimes."

"The sheriff was there. Isn't he your uncle? He hates my ass. He keeps asking when I'm going back to school."

"He never liked my mama." I didn't say that when Preston and Dale called him, Sheriff Evans saw my mother naked and bloody on the floor, his little brother dead outside. He did the math and he knew. He knew.

"Why didn't the sheriff like your mama?"

"He just didn't." I gave Henry another biscuit. "You know how folks get."

Dixie's bruises didn't fade before the funeral, and makeup caked around her eyes. Henry held my hand when we said we were sorry about Clint. Her mama hugged me around Clint Junior. "Didn't you see Dixie the morning Clint died?" Henry asked as we drove down Lost John Road.

"Yeah." Damn Shirley for talking when he could hear. "She wasn't feeling well. I sat with her for a while."

"What was wrong with her?"

"Sad, mostly," I said, which wasn't a lie. "You know how some women get after they have a baby, 'specially when their husbands drink too much." Goddamn him for noticing. My stomach flipped, and my toes curled in my black church shoes. Henry had to stop asking questions, 'cause he wouldn't like their answers.

By the time the swamp went green with spring, Henry sat with the younger men at the diner and hit the Roadhouse with them every night. He said they teased him for keeping to one beer. "But they say they'd run their asses down the road if they had you waiting for 'em, too," he told me.

I'd've seethed over that, but when we were thirteen, I'd knocked Randy out of an oak tree and kissed him afterward. At fourteen, I tricked Darryl into a thicket of poison ivy, then made it up to him in the back of his daddy's pickup. Dalton and I lost it together, and I still smiled over that. We remembered each other's missing teeth and broken arms and bee stings. They were mine. They were Lower Congaree.

"I've gotta get started on those stories," Henry said one night while we snuggled under warm blankets. "I'll lose my funding if I don't."

"Hush. I need to tell you something." I'd held her close for weeks, told her stories and sang her into staying. "You'll either be real happy or real mad." Henry might leave, or he might stick around. One way or another, Lower Congaree would catch fire with gossip. I prayed he wouldn't go, this man who brought me cookies, who kissed my cheek, who held my hand when we walked into Brewster's.

Henry turned enough to slip a hand onto my belly. "Right there," he whispered.

He took a leave of absence from Carolina.

LIKE ALL MEN'S FIGHTS, it was stupid from one end to the other. Randy started on Dalton. Dalton started on Randy. Randy got angry, so Dalton got angrier, and they took it outside. They started with punches, then Randy picked up a broken bottle. Dalton pulled out his Bowie knife. Maybe he forgot Randy had his concealed carry. Maybe he'd drunk himself dumb enough to think Randy wouldn't use it.

It only took one shot. Dalton's blood pooled in the hot summer dust. "Tell Ella Lee," he said as red trickled from his mouth.

Henry held him while he passed. Afterward he came home and held me while I cried. The child wept inside me.

"Why'd Dalton want someone to tell you?" he asked as he rubbed my back up and down, up and down. His shoulder was wet with my tears.

"Don't you worry about it," I managed between sobs.

"You can tell me, Ella Lee."

My sobs stopped fast. "Don't ask questions," I said, and walked out back. My babies saw my tears. I lifted my arms to them and whispered words Henry could never hear. They rose into dark as black as their wings.

A cop found Randy dead in the jail's exercise yard. Heart attack, said the coroner, maybe a stroke. Randy's eyes and tongue were missing.

That's how Sheriff Evans told it down at the diner. I was sitting right there, but my uncle didn't care—he wanted me to hear it. *I know what you did, Ella Lee*, he was saying. He thought my mama had killed his little brother, and he blamed me for it. But the sheriff was blood, and blood was untouchable.

"And there were crows all over that exercise yard," my uncle finished.

Henry squinted at him. "Say that again?"

"We found him with a flock of crows," my uncle said. "They didn't leave til we took his body away. Happened with Clint Booker, too. Ella Lee here, it happened with her daddy when we found him after that hurricane."

People shifted in their chairs. No one said much of anything after that. I couldn't finish my breakfast, and Henry told Dale he didn't feel well. The baby fluttered as Henry followed me home. He got out of his city-boy car and trailed into the house after me.

It was coming, sure as a summer storm. I could almost smell the ozone. The hairs on my neck rose, and our child kicked hard.

"I came up here looking for stories." Henry's voice shook. "You know them all."

I didn't answer.

"You don't go sit with women. That root cellar's not for cooking."

He'd always asked questions, and he'd always hated my babies. I should've known it would happen one day.

"You're the wise woman or the healer or the folk magician. Whatever they call you." Henry stepped back, one single shuffle. "You're the witch."

I stared him down. "Don't you call me a goddamn witch."

"They all know it. You wanted me because I didn't." Despite the heat, he wrapped his arms around himself. "You killed Randy 'cause he killed Dalton. You killed Clint 'cause he beat up Dixie. Those crows out there"—he pointed toward the trees my babies loved—"they tore out their eyes."

Damn my uncle to hell, 'cause I couldn't send him there myself.

Henry gestured at my belly. "And that's the next one."

"Maybe that's why I liked you at first. You didn't know." He'd caught me, and I couldn't hand him anything but the truth. "But it's more now."

"How do I know you didn't make me fall in love with you? It's fake. You made me feel this way."

"No." My voice caught. "Henry, I would never do that. Anything you feel is yours."

His boots slid on my wooden floor as he backed up again. "If I leave, you'll set your crows on me. I'm trapped here. I'm like a goddamn princess in a tower. You're a psychopath, and I just fathered another one. That's why the sheriff hates you. That's why, Ella Lee."

I tried to take his hand. Henry jerked back. "It's not like that," I told him. "I help—"

"You kill people," he shot back. "You decide who dies."

"They deserved it!" I shouted, and my babies rustled in their tree. "Henry, please." Our daughter kicked and punched. "Stop. I never did anything to you. I never made you stay, and I never made you fall in love with me. I could've, and I didn't. Someone here has to help people. Someone has to keep order—"

"That's not how it works!"

"That's how it works here, and it's always worked that way." My voice dropped low. "You came here for stories? That's your story, Henry. It's different here in the swamp, and it always will be."

"Now that I know, you'll never let me leave." Henry slammed out. "I know you now!" he shouted, and I ran onto the porch 'cause I knew what he was doing. It was stupid but inevitable as winter.

Staring up at my crows, Henry stood at the base of their tree. "I know you!" he yelled as they flapped and rustled. "Carrion eaters, all of you! I was right! I said it and I was right!"

Those crows hated him 'cause he hated them. "Don't!" I yelled, but it was too late. Still as stone, those crows burst suddenly to life, like they'd waited for that moment, like they'd known it would come, and they'd only bided their time.

Henry disappeared behind beating black wings. I couldn't stop them.

I screamed. Deep in my belly, our child screamed with me.

Babylon Burning

Whenever his children or his children's children or the children that came after clamored about the War, Townsend Trenholm remembered the pale, cautious sunshine of that January afternoon in 1865, when he was twelve, how it sidled through the bareblack branches above his cousin's cabin and seemed to bear in itself the scent of wet winter mud. The slaves had fled two days before. His grandmother said that hope of Sherman's invasion had finally ruined them, and when Cypress Bend rose at the thin, strangled crow of the last remaining rooster, the Trenholms found cabins gaped empty, storehouses looted to bare shelves, and shoals of barefoot prints leading from the quarters to the trackless wastes of Congaree's vast malarial swampland. Stray chicken feathers and hog prints dotted their trail. The tattered troop of Negros had stolen everything—*taken what was rightfully theirs,* Town would say a long time later, but then his grandmother called them thieves and wept bitter-righteous tears. *Didn't we give them everything we could,* she said. *This's how they pay us. Lookit that. You can't trust 'em. I always said you can't trust 'em and I was right, I was right all along.*

Two days after that rank treason, after a frantic scuttle to bury the family silver, Town's grandmother dispatched him to check that those Negros had not perpetrated unspeakable deeds upon wayward Cousin Sylvia and her bastard baby. Grandmother sent along with him the gardener, Town's second cousin Randolph, spared soldiering on account of his withered right hand. "A cripple and a boy," Randolph said as they left the lonely barnyard, neat as a tomb because there was nothing to do but keep it that way. "That's the best men that Cypress Bend can muster, 'cause all the rest are dead."

Like a schoolhouse rhyme, Town could have recited the Trenholm family losses: his brother Sully, killed at Second Manassas; Uncle Ashby, killed at Fredericksburg; his father Lyons, dead at Cold Harbor. His cousin Henry had not been seen since Gettysburg and they presumed him dead too. *I'm not a boy*, he could have told Randolph. *I'll fight Sherman if he gets close, you see if I don't.*

You're twelve years old, Randolph would have said, then he would have cut his iron-colored eyes sideways and added in a voice ugly as a blacksmith's rasp, *Skinny, too.* And Town would have been ashamed, so he kept silent and fingered the Stranger coin in his pocket, kept for luck though luck ran watery-weak. Maybe the slaves would find Strangers in the swamp.

Trenholm cousins whispered about them when their mothers were rolling bandages. *A strange, small man came covered in skins, and they said he spoke no language they'd ever heard of, like an Indian but he wasn't an Indian,* Cousin Lafayette had said, and Town resented the six months between them, how those two slim seasons lent his cousin a wisdom he could never touch.

Beyond fences splintered forlorn with dry-rot and pastures thick and high and brown because there was no stock to graze them, Town and Randolph passed onto the swamp path where wan sun laced through the branch filigree above. No birds sang, and in the winter chill, no mosquitoes bit. They slogged through soughs and guts and muck to Sylvia's cabin of rough-hewn cypress logs, which hunkered atop a clump of earth like an animal readying for winter.

"Quiet," Randolph said, which Town could not parse as command or observation. A poorly woven fence surrounded rabbit-nibbled collards and spinach greens; a wide and silent swamp stream curled into the distance beyond. Sunshine dappled the half-tamed cabin and its feral little barn. As he stood under that fragile light shining like lacework through the winter branches, Town suddenly and sickeningly recalled Sherman not forty miles off burning Orangeburg. When he finished the general would march on Charleston or Columbia or maybe Congaree.

"Don't hear that bastard of hers," Randolph said.

"His name's John." Town stepped to the window and knocked. Sylvia's single room contained unfashionable cast-offs from the main house, overlarge in the small space and ill-fit to rot in a steam-choked cypress swamp.

Back turned to Town, Sylvia was tucking a man-shape into the high tester bed shoved into a corner.

"I'm coming," she told him.

If Randolph saw the man-shape he would drag it from the bed and beat it; the holy and righteous moral fury of every female Trenholm would once again descend upon the unbowed dark head of his cousin Sylvia, already exiled to this hermetic swamp-outpost as punishment for her sins. Town scuttled to the door. "She's coming," he told Randolph. "She was just making the bed."

Sylvia stepped through the door with her baby in her arms. His eyes were overlarge for his face, but despite the pallor of ill nutrition he watched them with the bright curiosity of a fox cub. His cousins said he looked like Town and maybe he did. When Town reached for him, Sylvia passed him over.

"What were you doing in there?" Randolph asked.

"I was making the bed, like Town told you," Sylvia said.

"Grandmother sent us to check on you because the slaves ran away," Town told her. "They took all the food that wasn't stored in the main house. And Sherman's burning Orangeburg prolly right now. We had a rider come yesterday and tell us."

Taking up a pinestraw broom as if she could not waste even a moment with speech, Sylvia swept at the dirt, which did nothing that Town could see but stir up fine, ageless dust. "They raided the gardens?" she asked.

"They took everything," he replied.

"I'll send you home with collards," she said.

He opened his mouth to argue that she was alone with the baby and therefore needed the greens more than they did, since they had at least the canned foods in the pantry, when a wrenching, agonized moan erupted from the house.

"Who the hell was that?" Randolph hefted the wrist-thick, grayish cudgel hauled through two miles of rank swampland. Sylvia simply watched him. It was the same look Town remembered her giving his mother and grandmother when she stood in their airless front parlor, barefoot and bigbellied. Those blackclad women had battered her relentlessly as a rising storm tide, but Sylvia had shown no expression, no malice or sadness or sign of regret, but had simply gone on looking as if she was seeing not women but at some reflection of humanity itself. *She's insolent and slatternly*, Town's mother had said after, and Town had thought that was not quite right.

"I asked you what the hell that was," Randolph said again, which counted as one more insult against her because he did not apologize for his language in front of a lady and a child besides. "Who's in your house, Sylvia?"

But she only went on looking at him in that clearing under the hollow January sun. If Town sniffed hard and deep he imagined he could smell the smoke of a burning city forty miles off. The silver was buried deep. They had nothing else worth stealing but their dignity and maybe not even that anymore.

"You got one of them Negros in your house?" Randolph asked. "You tell me now and maybe I'll go easy on them."

Sylvia stayed still and silent as those winter trees. The baby in Town's arms did not squirm. Randolph shoved his cudgel into the door and pushed it open.

"No," Sylvia said quietly, and once only.

A string of blistering invective rose as Randolph stomped into the cabin. Town imagined muddy prints marring her clean wood, then heard a sick thump as that man hit the floorboards. "You got a goddamn Yankee in here!" Randolph shouted. "You traitor whore, you got a Yankee soldier in your bed!"

She shouted something like *he's not* and dashed into the house. Town set the baby in that fine-sifted dust. He sat up with his fat hands planted in the earth and his bright eyes the same shade as the high, cold sky. Town loved Sylvia. But he hated Yankees more, and he ran.

Muck sucked his feet, which had long worn out any shoes the world might have to offer, and since his brother's still flopped hopelessly, Town ran unshod through wet-splattering mud clotted thick with last year's leaf-skeletons, his coin clutched tight in his fist though he was too old to believe in it. *We're finished,* Mother had said. *My son doesn't have shoes to wear. I never thought I'd fall so far into that my son would have no shoes.* Smilax vine tore at his mended and tattering pants. His brother and father and uncle and cousin had flung themselves into the churning maul of war so Yankees would never come to Cypress Bend and now they had come anyway. When Town reached the main house he was nearly wheezing with exhaustion and maybe fear he would never admit to but he hurled himself onto the porch and threw open the door and shouted, *"Yankees!* Sylvia has a Yankee soldier in her house!"

In a farther room, his sisters and cousins screamed high, pure curdles of terror. A moment later his mother and his aunts Eleanor and Nelia fluttered in, still clutching homespun bandages, Grandmother behind. Rail-thin and blackclad, they moved in tandem, like a flock of crows. "Repeat yourself without hysteria, Townsend Trenholm," his grandmother ordered.

"We went to check on Sylvia like you said and she got a Yankee soldier in her house," Town said.

The old woman had held that plantation together for four years of loss and privation and her expression said that she would hold it through Judgment Day, against God Himself if necessary. "Just one?" she asked.

"Yes," Town told her.

"The Home Guard is too busy to deal with him," Grandmother said. "We'll have to take care of this ourselves."

"Mother, we don't have enough to keep a prisoner fed," Aunt Nelia told her.

Grandmother turned her head with the slow deliberation of a hunting owl. Town would remember that look forever, her eyes narrowing into something flinted and iron-hard that he had never seen. Not a day before she had told them to hide the silver under the manure pile because the Yankees would be too squeamish to check there, and when her daughter-in-law protested, she told her to pick up a shovel or forget about dinner. She had cried about the slaves but ever since something inside her had broken or perhaps come together in a kind of vicious strength Town had never imagined, and it frightened him. "We won't be feeding a prisoner," Grandmother told his aunt. "His people killed Sully and Lyons and Ashby, and Henry too."

Aunt Eleanor covered her face in her hands—they generally pretended there was some hope for Cousin Henry, since missing did not always mean dead—but the other women straightened. Grandmother had invoked their holy martyrs. "Keep rolling bandages. Randolph will bring him along. Townsend, there's plenty of firewood stacked around the cabins. You and Lafayette pile it under the Meeting Oak."

"Yessum." Town knew better than to ask questions. Since his grandmother had stopped crying, she granted no quarter and brooked no opposition; he would do it, and he would not ask why. Lafayette was mending a belt on the back veranda, his hound dog at his feet. He fed it on fox squirrel but it stayed bone-thin and hungry-mean. "Why d'you think we're piling wood?" he asked Town as they walked back to the cabins.

"I think she wants it all in one place so we can find it easy," Town said. Then, because for once there were no women or sisters or little brothers around, he asked, "Do you think the Negros will find any Strangers in the swamp?"

"Maybe," Lafayette said. "I wish I could see a Stranger."

"Where d'you think they come from?" Town asked.

Lafayette held hands out like he was praying or trying to pick up empty air. "Uncle Lyons, when he came home on leave last year, he said they're from Cypress Bend but before or after us. Like the coins. He thought Strangers were Trenholms too but I think that's wrong."

Town hated his cousin suddenly; his own father had told Lafayette something he'd never say to Town himself, and Father was dead for a cause that had done no good in the end. The Yankees had come anyway.

They cleaned out the cabins down to the kindling boxes, and that kept them busy 'til sunset fell in tattered pink and orange. They were cold-toed and chill-fingered when they finished. When they came back to the house Randolph was coming up to the bare-sticked front garden. He led their last ribby mule, and a limp man slung over its back like a sack. The man's pants and shirt were dirt-crusted and swamp-stained but their blue showed through in patches. Sylvia walked behind, the baby in her arms.

"He's not a soldier," she said when she saw Town.

"Sure's hell he is." Randolph jerked the rope. Hungry, exhausted on thin pasture, the mule flung its head with affronted pride but walked on. "You see that blue? She wants to save him."

"He has things in the woods that prove it," Sylvia said. "He buried them to keep them safe but when he's not delirious he can say where they are and show them to you. I have more in—"

"He's a Yankee," Randolph said.

"He's not," Sylvia told them. "He—"

Randolph turned and spit, an indictment that said everything about who Sylvia was and what she did against family and country and maybe even God Himself. "Shut up."

Town had a terrible idea, and he opened his mouth to say it but his grandmother swooped onto the porch with his mother and aunts, that old crow-flock alighting like a murder on a gravesite. The girls clustered behind them and the little boys peeped through their legs. "You brought him," Grandmother said. "Stand him up."

"He can't stand up," Sylvia said. "He's had ague for four days."

Grandmother stepped from the rest of the women. She had lost Grandfather just after Fort Sumter and her sons Ashby and Lyons to the great and grand Southern Cause that no longer seemed so great or so grand at all after four years of scrambling and starving and now hiding the silver under the manure pile. She had lost her grandson Sully and probably Henry, who went to war instead of college, and Town and Lafayette had no shoes. The girls had no fabric for dresses and the women no dye for mourning clothes; the slaves had run away and stolen the last of their meat, which they had no salt to preserve anyway. As the old woman stepped forward Town saw these outrages carved on her as if they had twisted her flesh and hewn his grandmother into more than herself, goddess-like in rage and pain and vengeance.

"How long has he been at your house?" Grandmother asked,

and in that long gray silence that came just before winter twilight, her voice was too quiet.

"Six days," Sylvia said. "I found him half-naked and starved in the swamp when I went out to look for wild ginger. He's not a soldier."

"Then why's he wearing that blue?" Grandmother demanded more than asked, and her tone brooked no disagreement, as if what she said was self-evident and could not be denied.

"He's from somewhere else," Sylvia said.

The man reared upright. Wild-eyed as a frightened horse, his buttoned shirt hung in strips, and he stared around him, gaping and confused. "Been here before but it's different," he said. "On a field trip. I had to write a report."

"A report!" Lafayette crowed. "He's a Yankee spy! He said it!"

"No!" Sylvia clutched the baby to her chest. But Grandmother was pointing toward the cabins. She was saying something to Randolph that Town could not make out over his cousin's pleas. The girls were in an uproar of terror that a spy should come to Cypress Bend, because one spy would beget more. His mother and aunts nodded, that crow-flock in solemn agreement with their leader, and then they were all marching down the muddy road toward the cabins with the man clinging to the mule and Sylvia crying and weeping behind, though her baby made no sound. Town knew better than to comfort her. Whatever monstrous energy had possessed Grandmother would only come down upon him if he dared to speak up on Sylvia's behalf. The man had said—but what if—two impulses warred in him and Town did not know which was correct. He knew only that he was twelve years old and blue twilight was falling fast as the night-cold crept in and tightened, tightened. He could not stand against four years of war and death and poverty and silver buried under the manure pile.

"Randolph, drive a sturdy pole next to that woodpile, man-height," his grandmother said when they reached the Meeting Oak. "Hold that mule, Town."

He had a terrible sick sense about something about to happen, trembling on the cusp of a deed too terrible to contemplate. Sylvia thrust the baby at him; Town grabbed for the child before it fell. Lafayette took the mule. Implacable as a god, Randolph drove a stake as the man babbled feverishly about a field trip and a report and a plantation visit. His skin shone pale in the blue-black dark and his eyes showed too much of their whites.

"The Home Guard is busy," his grandmother said. "We're going to take care of this ourselves. I won't waste bullets on a Yankee. We'll burn him like they burn our cities."

"He's not from here!" Sylvia shouted. "I'm telling you—"

"You're a liar and a whore and we don't believe whores in this house." Grandmother's voice took command of the fields and humped buildings and long-falling twilight, like Town imagined God would sound, His vengeance and His anger. She demanded this single sick man as recompense for the sins of a whole Babylon. He had killed no Trenholm, but she would not be swayed, and Town knew better than to try. He clenched his coin tight. *I will not cry I will not cry I will not cry*, he told himself, because he was twelve years old and he would shame himself, even if Randolph was dragging the man from the mule. The gardener yanked the man by his wrists, and his head and heels slammed the unvictorious dirt. His face raked through the firewood, spilling it everywhere, as Randolph shunted him upright and lashed him to the stake.

"Town! Lafayette! Pile that wood up right!" Grandmother pointed imperiously as one of the Furies themselves. From sheer habit of obedience, Town gave Sylvia the baby. All panic gone, she wore that dark-eyed look he remembered from the parlor. "Leave now," she told him. "Or you'll remember this for the rest of your life, and you've seen enough already."

Randolph was tying the man's chest to the stake. He moaned low and desperate, a deep-sea creature heaved on a beach. Town and Lafayette scrabbled at his feet like beetles and heaped up the wood. He remembered his mother reciting the verse: *Then they will weep and wail at the sight of the fire that consumes her, Babylon—Woe, woe to the great city, your hour has come*

Town could not break away from that fragment, repeated again and again in his mind's white silence, his mother's voice, as if in this strange extremity his mind clung to the known and familiar. His grandmother held a box of Lucifer matches, and as she strode down the porch steps she seemed in the gathering dark to be too tall and too broad to be a woman. The man's eyes had closed. He slumped, as if in his sickness he had given himself over to her. Vestal, beautiful in a vengeance indiscreet, Grandmother knelt and struck the match.

Town ran.

His feet slapped the mud and for the second time that day, he ran down that swamp path. He held the coin tight, tight, almost certain then and terrified in his certainty, ignoring the smilax thorns that lashed his pants and the black swamp pressed on every side, unknowable and unsettled. Behind him, screams rose like the smoke of a burning city. Town understood as he bolted through that forest that his grandmother had burnt—was burning, the man was screaming and he was burning—she was burning that man as one final act of revenge against a world that stole away her sons and her slaves and the social order she believed in blood and bone and body and soul.

Those thin high screams of undeath trailed Town until he was no longer sure if he heard them or supplied them in his own grim fearful certainty. He ran until his breath jerked in his lungs and wheezed in his throat, until his palms slammed the roughwood door of his cousin's cabin and he shoved inside. The coals were still burning, and on the table next to the bed he found what he was looking for, what he dreaded: three coins. *United States of America,* they read. *In God We Trust.* And the dates: *1981, 1983, 1986.* And a strange cylinder, made of some white material he'd never seen, with a blue cap on one end. When he took the cap off, the pointed end smeared his finger blue, and he realized it was a miraculous kind of pen.

Holding his own coin tight, Town dropped to the floor next to that cast-off bed in the small swamp-cabin, trying not to cry for all he'd lost, because girls cried and babies cried and he was neither. Town failed. *The war will make you strong,* his father had said as he rode out of Cypress Bend, out of Lower Congaree, into the world of men and blood, smoke and madness. *Sylvia has a Yankee soldier in her house,* he had shouted to his grandmother, his mother and sisters, his aunts. Sylvia had said he wasn't and why didn't Town believe her?

Because Sully and Father and Uncle Ashby and Cousin Henry are gone, he thought. They are gone and didn't Father say to take care of Mother and the girls while he was off fighting Yankees? Didn't he? Didn't he say that he left so no Yankee could ever come to Cypress Bend and tell us what to do?

Back bumped against the wall of rough logs, Town curled on the clean-swept floor in the breathless winter dark. Duty had not driven him through that swamp to tell them about the Yankee soldier. He had run because Sherman was coming, because Orangeburg was burning, because if he ran they would talk about him like they talked about Father and Uncle Ashby and Sully and Henry. His furious sprint would make up those two scant seasons between him and Lafayette, and then Cousin Randolph would no longer cut his metal-colored eyes sideways and tell Town he was skinny.

Father had said a man was measured by the size of his actions. Town had gotten someone killed and what could be bigger than death? He curled tighter and cried harder. *I don't want it,* he sobbed, to the cabin, to the swamp, to his cousin who would come back soon with the bastard baby whose father she knew better than to name, because they would not believe who put him in her belly—he knew that too, a sudden stricken knowledge that choked him breathless. His mother also knew, and Sylvia never said it because they would not believe her. They couldn't.

I don't want it, Town wept. I don't want it. I don't want it. This is not what they said. This is not what it's supposed to mean.

But it does, he would tell his children and his children's children. It does.

For Thine Is the Kingdom

His oldest died first. Jubal Early Rowell IV, called Four by everyone but his mother, spent a late night swigging moonshine with the Lanier boy, then picked up his car keys. He might've died of blood loss, the coroner said, or he might've died of a brain injury, or maybe he passed out before he hit that cypress tree, a mercy. Jubal Early Rowell III identified his nineteen-year-old son's broken body and left the morgue for death's other offices.

They sweated through his funeral on one of the hottest days of summer. Men went red faced in dark suits; women waved fans from Lower Congaree's only funeral home. The closed casket told everyone what Four looked like sure as if they'd parked him downtown as a freak show.

Jubal remembered her as they threw dirt on his son's casket. She'd come on a day near as hot as that one, walked barefoot off the road and down his curving driveway of live oaks. Beyond them, his long, flat tobacco fields had grown thick and high and ready for harvest; hired hands were cleaning out the curing sheds. A maid saw her coming and said, "It's that Winters girl. She's 'bout to ring the bell, Mister Rowell."

He met her on his white, columned porch before she got a chance. He'd intimidate her, and she'd go away: simple. No more than fifteen, and a young fifteen at that, she wore a dirty dress and clutched two pale children the spit and image of Four. He claimed not to know her, even if everyone in Lower Congaree knew her. But he was Jubal Early Rowell III, not some backwoods tenant farmer, and he could pretend. "What happens to my baby'll happen to you and yours," she'd said.

But no. The world didn't work like that.

His daughter Bertie went next—childbirth. The midwife, Jane Merle, said every birthing woman walks a knife's edge, and some fall. They buried Bertie with her baby. Her husband, who came from trash, named it Rudolph Farrow Junior, no middle name because he didn't have one.

Women died in childbirth. Jane said so, and everyone agreed Jane knew things better than most—women said she could help the hopeless, but that was as much superstitious nonsense as that skinny girl's ranting. Only coincidence that Bertie passed one year to the day after Four. Coincidence, nothing more.

Bertie's husband drank himself to death. By then they had Bertie's little Alice with them, and Jubal loved her best. She might've been called Farrow but everyone agreed she was a Rowell from top to toe. She'd tour the farm with him, her stout white pony keeping pace with his Tennessee Walker. "Granddaddy," she asked as they trotted along a field's edge, the sun high and hot and white, "if I live with you do I get to be Rowell now?"

"You should be," he told her. "You can mind your manners, eat without scraping your fork, ride sidesaddle, and put a bullet through a running rabbit's eye. You're eight years old and I oughta buy you a bigger pony for your birthday."

Alice pursed her little lips, then said, "I want a stallion like yours."

"Little girls are too small for stallions."

She fixed him with a glare he could've seen in the mirror if he cared to look, those narrow green eyes, that long, slightly scrunched nose. "I want a real horse."

"Don't be ugly, Alice," Jubal told her.

The next morning, his own black Tennessee Walker appeared at the barn gate with broken reins trailing in the dirt and a man's saddle on its back. After two frantic hours of sweat and worry, they found Alice in the far field. She wore a pair of pants she'd stolen from the maid's boy, and her open eyes stared blind at the sun.

Jubal refused to leave his room for weeks. That skinny girl's face, pinched and hungry, mocked him every time he closed his eyes. She'd stood barefoot on his spotless white porch, a baby in each arm. Neither had cried or whimpered and their heads seemed too big for their bodies. "You know whose babies these are," the girl said, flicking blondish hair from her forehead. "This one here, he's sick. I only want what's mine."

Men like him didn't deal with low-class chippies like her. "Get off my porch," Jubal ordered. "I don't know those babies from Adam's housecat."

She cussed a blue streak. Her spit landed on his shiny white bucks, and before he'd recovered from that horror, she said, "I only want what's mine. You think my babies are trash and trash don't deserve to live. You look and see where that trash came from. You look. What happens to my baby'll happen to you and yours."

What if—but life didn't run in simple patterns; words spoken didn't build a world. Bad things happened, and a man lived with them. He didn't go blaming some slip of a thing who'd come round to his front door—not even the back!—and battered him with crazy talk after she spit at his feet.

Lucas went the year after. Leukemia, the doctors said, caught too late. A long death, and an ugly one. His boy went screaming.

Delia, his youngest, caught influenza. Influenza slipped to pneumonia. She passed at a cold hospital surrounded by machines, and they knew she'd died because the machines stopped beeping. "Jane could've helped her," his wife said. "We should've had Jane come."

"Nothing Jane could've done the hospital didn't," Jubal told her.

"What d'you know?" Lula asked. "You don't know."

Four, then Bertie and her baby Rudolph Jr., then Alice. Lucas and Delia, and Rudolph Farrow if a person counted him, which Jubal sometimes did and sometimes didn't. All four children and two grandchildren, dead in a span of six years.

You help my baby—I only want what's mine. You know who he belongs to and I'll have my rights, I swear to God I will. He'd told her to go to hell. Those babies belonged to Four sure as if his son had said so, but goddamn if Jubal would admit it. Boys will be boys and those things happened. You didn't bring them 'round to the front door.

Three weeks after Delia passed, in a dining room gone gold with morning light, Jubal wondered why Lula was sleeping so late—she woke with the sun to drink black coffee and harangue the cook. "Bella," Jubal said to the maid, "go see what Lula's about."

Bella slid upstairs. A minute later she screamed and he knew.

Died of a broken heart, said everyone in Lower Congaree. Lost her sons, lost her daughters, lost her grandbabies and couldn't stand to look at the world anymore. Jubal stood silent as they lowered her into that cold earth on the darkest day of the year. He refused to cry in front of God and everyone, and he succeeded, mostly. That family plot was full, too full, only room for him now under that brown grass but who else was left?

I only want what's mine.

You look. What happens to my baby'll happen to you and yours.

He raised his eyes as the preacher who thought too much of himself, dragging out the Lord's Prayer. And goddamn if that girl, still string-bean skinny, wasn't staring at him from across his wife's open grave. The blond boy at her side studied him.

"Who the hell do you think you are?" Jubal roared.

"For thine is the kingdom..." died in the preacher's throat. People whipped around to stare.

"Get out!" Jubal shouted. "Get out and don't come back!"

She was already gone.

There was no such thing as a curse. He repeated it as they walked him into the church, sat him down in a vestibule, and handed him a glass of water. "No such thing as a curse," he told them, even as their faces went blurry. He only saw hers, her sharp nose, her blue-gray eyes, her thin lips. "There's no such thing as a curse."

They put him to bed for a week. But what could he do? A man had to go on living. He got up eventually, got up bitter, but got up nonetheless. And when his tobacco failed every year, he cussed and found an excuse. *Not enough rain. Too much rain. Lazy fieldhands. Late frost.* Jubal clung to those excuses even as the Laniers and the Trenholms pulled in record crops. But they had better soil. Better fieldhands. Better seed. Good seed meant everything.

Servants didn't stay long, and eventually he couldn't afford them. Mary Joiner came in to cook, and Jubal lived alone in that house full of echoes.

He should've been a patriarch then, reigning on high from the head of a dinner table. Instead he ate alone in the kitchen and his beard grew white and wild. The children and grandchildren were gone. What was a life without a legacy? Blood was everything, and he had no blood left.

But maybe something could be done. Something. Anything. And if anyone could do it, Jane Merle could. Women said she cured sickness, and maybe a curse was a kind of sickness. He didn't leave the property anymore, but he asked Mary Joiner to bring Jane over.

"What d'you want with Jane Merle?" Mary asked.

"I want to talk to her is all."

"Nothing you need to talk to Jane about," Mary said, still focused on her cooking.

"Not your business if there is or there isn't, you bring her over here," Jubal told her, and some of the old power came back into his voice.

That evening, as he watched the sun set from his porch rocker, Jane walked up his drive. It had long gone to deep ruts with crabgrass grown up between them; scrub brush and thorned smilax crowded the live oaks. Jane didn't speak until she'd climbed his steps. "What seems to be troubling you?" she asked, as if they'd met on the street, as if he wasn't barefoot or wearing a stained shirt.

"I'm cursed," Jubal said.

"No such thing."

He squinted into the sun. "Don't you lie to me."

"Who cursed you, then?" she asked.

He told her about that skinny girl and her two babies. "You didn't help her," Jane said.

Jubal looked at that sun setting, the long dark shadows crowding too close. "I chased her off."

"Whose babies were they?"

"They were Four's. I knew it then and I know it now." It took all his pride to say it, but he had no cause for pride, not anymore. "You know what happened after. They're all dead. My tobacco won't grow and my servants won't stay and hell, my damn horse colicked and died. I dream about her every night. It's a curse and I heard you can lift curses." A little lie wouldn't hurt. "I'll give anything."

Jane handed him a hard glare.

"Anything, I swear. I want peace."

"You tell me that girl's name first."

Jubal had tried hard to forget and he'd never said it, not once. "Winters. It was that Winters girl. Will you lift it now? I just want peace."

"Write her name down first. And write down whose babies they were. I won't do it otherwise."

Jubal heaved himself from his rocker. His knee ached, but he found an old receipt and wrote it down: *Caddy Winters's babies belong to Four.* Everything had narrowed to one point, one simple sentence. He'd denied his own blood and there was no greater sin. A man who refused his own blood deserved nothing in this world or the next. He'd killed them all, every one, sure as if he'd used a knife and his own right hand.

He gave Jane that old receipt.

Jane took it without a word. When he sat again, she laid a hand on his forehead. He felt it like a sigh, a settling. Jubal blinked into that sun going down. "Thank you," he murmured.

Jane said something about a judge, then she walked away holding that paper. Jubal's eyes closed. He welcomed what was his.

A Living Pentecost

Plump berries as long as Anna's thumb tempted in thorned tangles behind Ebenezer Galilee Church of Christ. Sour-sweet, those blackberries would burst on her tongue if she bit them. Her lips would purple; her tongue would turn black. A year ago, Isaiah had found them. They'd fed them to each other first, but in the end they were red-stained, once sticky-sweet but kissed clean.

No ma'am, he'd said five months later, gaze unwavering. *Not me.*

The white revival tent smothered Lower Congaree's hot-slopped summer night. Anna shifted from her left foot to her right. Her mother insisted on bringing her. *If anyone needs saved it's you,* she'd said.

> *. . . One day when sin was black as could be*
> *Jesus came forth to be born of a virgin,*
> *Dwelt among men, my example is he!*

. . .

Always virgins. Anna had tried to hide her growing belly, but that secret didn't keep. They called it God's judgment, and when that swelling in her belly turned to blood running down her thighs, they said that death was God's punishment. She could only abide. Anna liked the word, which meant both *to wait*, and *to endure*. She waited and she endured, and one day, she would leave everything behind.

Isaiah watched the preacher sing of a guilty heart. Anna swayed as if the Spirit moved her. Darkness dropped instead; it seethed like snakes. Under those blown-bright lights, where bugs slammed and buzzed in the deepening night, Pastor Wheeler, Isaiah's father, spoke over the organ. "Really feel the Spirit," he said. "It's a Pentecost now, when the Holy Spirit descended upon the Apostles as tongues of flame. You are a living Pentecost, my friends." He lifted his voice, and Anna sang with the rest. They started to fall, men and women, fall and babble as if gibberish was holiness. Why didn't the Spirit reach down and save her? Why didn't it punish Isaiah?

Her anger felt small and puny, a lump in her throat and an ache in her chest. It could not stand up to the forces arrayed against her. Anna abided, waited and endured—wasn't that a woman's lot, like Pastor Wheeler always said? But as she held that anger, it spread and bloomed against the singing. Rage ripened on the notes like buds on a vine, tendrils spread like kudzu, fast-growing, swallowing. People around her wept and babbled of God's love and Holy Fire but the ferocious fury that seized Anna had nothing to do with holiness. Her rage had a terrible beauty, and Anna gave her best self to it. Around her they fell with the Spirit.

Behold, she sang, *the fire from heaven falls.*

Anna's anger burst into blinding flame.

Babbling became screams. Burning should hurt but that fire blazed pure and holy. To burn was to be beautiful. There was divinity in that burning, clarity. Love. Folding chairs fell around her, but the Spirit was not forgotten. The Spirit was in her. Anna shouted in flame-tongued glory.

Isaiah tried to run. Anna caught him and laid her hands upon his head. His skin dribbled as holy flame ate him to nakedness, then black bone. Isaiah burned on a pyre of justice that lunged up like laughter.

Anna soared into smoke. In darkness, in righteousness, she ascended.

Folded in Light

"Most people couldn't make out what David was babbling when he ran outta that swamp. Partly 'cause he was buck-naked, but mostly 'cause he'd sawed off that hand. But I heard him." Buddy planted his elbows on the old counter. "He was going on about black rocks and witch birds and sacrifice. I know it. I seen it."

Blake had only stopped to top off at Lower Congaree's Gas N Go, but Buddy's gossip snagged him, and he leaned close. The clerk's Skoal reeked sickly of mint tobacco.

"David came in here telling me you can see those hunger stones in Germany," Buddy continued. "And those standing stones in Spain. He said that sure as shit the water level's dropping in that swamp. You think there isn't something back there? And I said, you come get me when you find it."

Buddy added that last detail like David's sawn-off hand wasn't enough, and Blake fumbled for cash. He'd be marked tardy at school if he lingered.

Congaree High roiled with rumor. Gossip peaked during lunch when most kids ate outside on splintered picnic tables. Staked trees drooped a dark, exhausted green, and the concrete courtyard sucked heat and held it. Blake contemplated his sandwich. The twin miseries of temperature and talk killed his appetite.

"He was so bloody that at first they didn't realize he was naked," Isabelle Gray said from a nearby table.

"Bullshit," said Blake's best friend Maddox, barely glancing at her. "You can't miss a swinging dick."

"You could if it's covered in blood!"

"A dick's a dick." Maddox fixed his big, dark eyes on Blake. Girls went crazy over those eyes. Maddox ignored them, and they went crazier. "I wanna know what he saw out there."

A slice of meat hung like a tongue from Blake's sandwich. "Maybe he snapped."

"David pulled straight As and Carolina scouted him for a baseball scholarship. No way would he up and lose it." Maddox's voice dropped low. "I think he really found—whatever drove him nuts."

"I bet he did," Evelyn Benson said from next to him.

Blake shoved his lunch away. He knew how it would happen then. Mad would say, *I have this great idea.* Blake would reply, *That's a terrible ide*a. Then Mad would tell him, *Evelyn's doing it,* and Blake would agree to his dumbass plan because he couldn't wuss out in front of Evelyn. Their usual trio had shifted into something Blake couldn't quite trust. None of them discussed it.

The sun shone red behind Blake's lids. "You're going to ask, and I'll argue," he said, "but I'll end up doing it, so let's not bother. I'll go into that goddamn swamp with you two. When? Saturday? You wanna go Saturday?"

Maddox might have smiled, or maybe his nose wrinkled into confusion. Blake didn't look. "Why not skip and go tomorrow?" he asked.

"And how'd you know I'd come?" Evelyn said.

When Blake finally opened his eyes, Maddox's head tilted. He seemed so intent on an answer. "I just knew," Blake replied.

"So, what're we doing?" Blake asked after he parked at the Gas N Go. "Are we taking a trail, or. . .?"

"Ask Mad." Evelyn's red hair hung long and loose; her hiking pants and boots suited a long tramp through the swamp, but her low-cut tank top didn't. Blake tried not to notice. "It's his idea." She grabbed her daypack from the seat.

"There's a deer trail around here," Maddox said as he slammed his door. "I thought we'd follow that and mark our way as we went along." He pawed through his pack, then held up a can of spray paint. "And yeah, I brought extra."

"I've got enough bug spray for all of us." Evelyn stepped away, and Blake backed up as Deet stung his nose. "I figured you delinquents would forget it."

Don't go into the swamp. It was a childhood commandment in Lower Congaree, as known as the other ten and probably better obeyed. Folks said snakes out there grew thick as a man's thigh. Gators sunk down in the muck, old gators, deadly gators, and feral hogs would strip a man to bone. But something else lurked there, and it was that something else older kids warned about. It watched, they said, and it waited.

No real trails led to the deep swamp.

Blake stayed silent as they walked toward the tree line.

A low, early fog promised another hot day. As birds tuned up, Maddox edged along the woods' weedy beginnings. He stopped at a gap between two bald cypresses.

"This is it, I think." He pointed to brown splatter staining the left tree's pale trunk. David had slapped his stump against it.

"Oh God, Mad, did you have to?" Evelyn made a face. "I could've lived without that."

"Whatever. C'mon." Maddox strode into the swamp. Evelyn went behind him, and Blake tried to keep up. Their path stayed faint, mostly dried mud churned by animals' feet and matted with dead leaves. Most brush had browned in the heat, but thorned smilax tore at them. After twenty minutes, blood beaded on their hands, and they hiked with their fists balled. Poison ivy twisted in hairy vines. Maddox stomped hard to scare off canebrake rattlers as he marked their trail. When they'd nearly lost sight of their last blaze, he sprayed another.

Blake didn't mention, and if she noticed, neither did Evelyn, that Maddox wasn't tracing hints of game trails. He followed bloodstained tree trunks.

As they roamed deeper, as the sun rose higher and their phones lost all bars, insects buzzed and hummed, rising to a whirring shriek. Flies bit, despite their Deet. *It wants our blood*, Blake wished he could say. But Maddox and Evelyn would have laughed and asked what, exactly, he meant. Blake couldn't have answered, *I mean the swamp. The swamp wants our blood*. Then they would've laughed harder.

Evelyn knelt. "Deer tracks," she said. "Maybe hogs. And I'd say that's a dog but it's too big."

"C'mon," Maddox called. "Blake, you okay back there?"

"Yeah, sure," he said.

More brown stains. The birds hushed. Blake smelled mud, a reek of silt rotting in the sun. When their faint trail disappeared or split, Maddox would pause and scan the swamp, sometimes meandering forward a bit. Then he'd shout, "This way!" and they'd catch up.

Maddox was searching for David's blood. Evelyn had to know.

Blake's neck prickled. When he whirled, three crows exploded from a swamp tupelo's branches in a raucous fury of caws.

"Goddamn, that scared me!" Evelyn clutched her fists to her chest.

Maddox huffed. "Stupid crows."

The insects quieted around noon, and Blake's neck went cold again. He peeked behind him. Three crows again, all watching them. "It's too quiet out here, y'all," he finally whispered.

"Yeah, 'cause nothing's stupid enough to be out in the middle of the day." Maddox threw him a lopsided grin.

But that hush seemed more than the silence of heat-wracked woods. Too many trees looked lightning struck. Too many thin, grub-pale mushrooms bloomed in the shadows. Didn't mushrooms need rain? Turkey-tail fungus fanned on fallen logs—not striped turkey-tail, but flat black. Occasionally, dry cane rattled. There was no wind.

"We should go back," Blake said.

"We're not going back now," Maddox replied over his shoulder.

"Why, Mad?" Evelyn spoke too loudly. "'Cause the bloodstains are getting worse?" Crows burst from a treetop: one, two, three of them. "I don't wanna find it. I don't wanna know what did it."

Maddox halted, then faced them. "So why'd you come?" He held her glare.

"If she'd rather go back—" Blake began.

"Oh, so you wanna go with her." Maddox gathered himself up like he did when they were little, like he was tired of playing a game. He stalked off. "Fine!" he called over his shoulder.

Evelyn crossed her arms tight. "If we let Mad go alone, he'll end up like David."

"Yeah." Blake blew out a long breath. "He will." No matter what was going on with the three of them—even if Evelyn picked Maddox instead of him—Blake couldn't let Mad face whatever was waiting alone. "C'mon, then."

Bald cypress knees stretched taller, taller, until they stood chest high. Maddox, Evelyn, and Blake trudged into land that had clearly lain submerged before the drought. As their trail twisted, they stepped into a clearing. Dark silt had cracked into hexagons, and a double circle of black standing stones gleamed with tiny, pitted crystals. Several stones were missing, shattered, or split. Those maimings pained Blake. Like ruined teeth between lovely lips, their ravage seemed worse for the beauty around them—a stark, strange beauty; the dry, sublime glory of earth and stone and sky.

It was nothing Blake had ever expected.

Knowing it was futile, he stepped up to a heap of broken stone and tried to fit its pieces together. The sun beat high and hot. A sole cricket sang. The stone was far taller than he, and long crumbled. "I can't fix it!" Blake shouted.

A crow landed in his shadow. "Fix it, fix it," the bird chanted.

Behind him, next to him, Evelyn and Maddox were working to fix stones, too. Blake collapsed onto split-silt dirt. "I just came out here because you wanted me to." His voice caught. "I came because you said she was coming, so I had to." He forced himself up. He had to help this single perfect stone.

"I came because you asked me," Evelyn was saying to Maddox somewhere behind him. Was she sobbing? "If you ask I have to say yes."

"I asked because Blake wouldn't come without you!"

Blake nearly stopped to look at Maddox, but his work was too important. Mad was weeping. Maybe his tears, like Blake's, fell on stone.

"It's the only way I can be around Blake," Mad was saying, as if the stones had broken him into hard, flinted truth, long hidden. "It's not that I don't like you, I do, I love you, but I love Blake too— I have to pick, it can't be both, and Blake, I—"

The stone wouldn't fit. The stone would never fit. Blake's scraped hands stung. A bloody knife lay on the ground, but it meant nothing to him now.

"I love you both," Maddox wept. "I can't pick."

Why hadn't Blake known? Being with Mad would be good— different, and a little scary because it was different, but still good. It had never occurred to him. "Why doesn't anything ever go together? It never goes together!" Blake kicked the shattered stone away and faced the circle's center.

"What are you doing?" Evelyn gasped, a short, sharp sound. "You can't do that! You'll ruin it!" Did she mean the stone? Did she mean *them*? Both?

The sun, once so punishing, folded Blake into its light. He could be part of something. The useless scrambling would end. Blake understood everything in a sudden flash bright as light catching stone. "It drove David insane, but he was alone. If we do it together, everything will fit." He began to undress.

"Yes," Maddox said, shucking off his shirt, and Blake knew that he understood, too.

Tears streaked the stone-dust on Evelyn's face. "What are you two talking about? What's this have to do with David?"

Maddox picked a rock so far gone it seemed pulverized. "Here. Evelyn, C'mon. David was alone so it made him crazy. But we're not."

Scuttling upright, her back hit a cypress knee on the garden's edge. "Don't!" she shouted as Blake strode toward the center, toward Maddox. "Blake, don't! Don't take him away!"

"Aren't you tired of that?" Blake couldn't stop for long. Maddox was waiting. "Don't you want it to end? C'mon. It'll end, right now."

"Don't!" Blood caked her broken nails. It was almost as dark as David's. "You'll ruin everything!"

Evelyn's grasping wouldn't let her see. Turning from her, Blake took Maddox's hands. Maddox smiled wide as he pulled Blake close. Skin to skin, feet to earth, they fit against each other. Far away, a person screamed. Slowly, in stillness and wonder, they shifted from that stubborn resistance of flesh. To become was beautiful, to fit sublime; they joined not only their sibling-stones but each other. Time slipped. If they ever looked back to their other life, it was with puzzlement. Stones knew no loneliness or fear. What was uncertainty to the earth? Sun warmed them. Rain bathed them.

Water returned. In love, in union, the stones waited.

Ink Vine

I counted my night's haul in the wan gas station light. Stiff and mint-new, the two hundred in twenties smelled crisp, the clean scent of untouched money. The ones and fives varied from ATM-sharp to flannel-soft. I liked to think about those old bills, where they'd been and who might've used them. I imagined little kids ordering soda, noses poking above convenience-store counters, or old men shuffling through a pharmacy line. I tried to ignore the reality of back pockets and sweaty palms. Customers sucked.

Two hundred and eighty—a middle kind of take-home, good for a Wednesday. I stuffed all but ten into my purse. Bugs hummed as I strode through the hot-breathed summer night. Damn global warming. Rich people and their private jets would kill us all, sweat us to death in the meantime. After a sweltering night at the club and a twenty-minute drive without air conditioning, my hair stuck to my neck. I'd have chopped it to my shoulders if I could, but my best friend, Alyssa McAllister, she swore guys liked long hair. "Then they can think about pulling it," she'd say, and I'd make a face. She didn't have to say it made me look younger, not that I didn't look seventeen already, and guys liked that even better. Barely legal dancers made the most money. It's ick, but life is ick all over. You'd think you'd get used to it, but you never do.

The Gas N Go's cowbell clanged in the four-thirty a.m. quiet, and Zeke glanced up from his porno mag. "Lookit you, Emmy Joiner," he said. I tried not to wince at my name in his mouth as he flicked greasy hair from his forehead. "You take a few minutes, you can earn some extra cash."

I didn't want to blush. The ugly light washed my skin white, and he'd see. "Pack of Parliament Lights, please."

"What's with you?" He made no move toward the cigarettes. "You'll fuck strangers, let alone those asshole McAllister boys, but you got none for me? I known you your whole life."

"I asked for a pack of Parliaments," I said. We stepped through the same crap every night I stopped in, but Lower Congaree shut down at eight. Unless I wanted to wait til eleven a.m., when Party Town #3 opened, I was SOL.

"I asked you to step out back with me." Zeke's face twisted into a leer. "Or we can take a minute in the bathroom. I ain't particular."

I gathered up my last shreds of courage. "I'm a dancer, not a whore, and I got cousins bigger and meaner than you. Pack of Parliament Lights, please." I kept my hands below the counter so he didn't see them shake. Six months ago, the daycare center downtown closed, and I started working at that club. In a week, the whole town knew, and Zeke had been hassling me ever since.

He flipped the cigarettes onto the counter. When I passed him cash, he held it to his nose and smirked.

"Those bills were nowhere near anything fun, you sick bastard." Eyes down, I snagged my cigarettes and fled. Fuck the change. Zeke would only keep harassing me, and it wasn't worth the time or two-fifty.

My old Nissan sputtered, then caught. It would die soon, and twice I'd blown my get-out-of-town money fixing it. Where would I find enough cash for a new car? I wouldn't, and no one would drive me to the club—Mama and Aunt Tabby would make me work at the chicken plant. I lit a cigarette and tried not to think about it. Everyone tells you not to smoke, but there's not much good in the world, and you gotta snatch happy where you can. Rich people think they know best. They don't know anything. Try being poor. See how much your feet hurt. Poor people sweat to death 'cause they can't afford to fix their air conditioners, and they come home from work stinking like chicken poo. You'd smoke too, if only to kill the smell.

I pulled outta the parking lot. The swamp sang on every side, all insect chitter and tree frog screech. Lower Conagree's only traffic light blinked red. Downtown was deader than dead, quiet as a tomb and just as creepy. Empty storefronts stood out like missing teeth. When I was in high school, we'd walk from the Gas N Go to Party Town #3, then pay whatever homeless guy hung outside to buy us liquor. He'd always do it 'cause we were cute, and me and Alyssa would cart it to the Lot and get plowed. She was so pretty, all long, pale legs and blonde hair. She smelled like roses, too. Sometimes we'd sit too close, cramming into a pickup truck or someone's backseat, and I'd try not to think about it.

I couldn't tell Zeke what I really thought: *I like girls better, and even if I wanted a guy, it wouldn't be a miserable counter-jockey like you.* He'd only say something like, *I know what can cure you of that*, and that gas station was real empty at four a.m. Not that I'd ever been with a girl. Bi women in Lower Congaree knew enough to keep quiet.

Zeke didn't know the truth, but he harassed me anyway. I was a broke-ass Joiner. White-trash welfare queens, that's what everyone called us, and so what if most of my family needed SNAP to get by? Born poor, stay poor. There aren't any bootstraps to pull up or ladders to climb, not if you're a Joiner kid. We lived in trailers and worked under the table or at the chicken plant, always had. I could threaten Zeke with my cousins, but they were too sorry and too stoned to care about shit-talking. He knew it, too.

I left town's sad emptiness and pulled onto the swamp road. At least guys liked me. They panted after my blue eyes and long legs, and they figured a Joiner girl would do anything for a few bucks. I raked in more money when they tried for it, but I hated cashing in on my own poverty. *Even if you're not a whore, you gotta act like one*, Alyssa always told me. *If they think they have a chance, they'll keep handing you bills.* The wind snatched my hair and whipped it into tangles. One more time, I wished I could cut it off.

Aunt Tabby's trailer clung to a weedy patch of ground on the edge of the swamp, and three broke-down old cars hunched in its drive like guilty dogs. I parked in the yard and shuffled through the grass, careful for snakes. Mama couldn't make rent alone. She and Aunt Tabby got up at dawn to work at the Bessinger Poultry Plant, where they plucked chickens and tried not to get their fingers stuck in machines. My fifteen-year-old brother Jett went to summer school at nine, or not, depending on his mood. I loved him more than all the rest of them put together. 'Cause of me, he had new clothes, nice shoes, and money for lunch; damn if the other kids would laugh at him like they'd laughed at me.

You don't have to do that, Emmy, he'd say.

Hush up and take it, I'd tell him.

He didn't want them to laugh either, so he'd nod and take lunch money, or the earbuds, the new shoes I'd picked up on a special trip to Columbiana Mall, thirty miles and a world away.

My sister Diamond slept in. Six months pregnant, she was miserable with morning sickness, afternoon sickness, evening sickness—if I ever needed a reason to swear off guys, she gave me a damn good one. Diamond had worked in the chicken plant til she barfed all over a plucked hen. That's how she knew she was pregnant. Ever since, money was tighter. With one person unemployed, I could hardly save enough for gas and cigarettes. But there was no way around it. You did what you could with what you had.

My cousin Jackson lived with us til Aunt Tabby kicked him out. She said he'd end up dead or in prison, and we didn't need a drug bust in our lives. Jackson bought weed from Talitha Merle's swamp garden and sold it at a fifty-percent markup, still cheaper than that shit coming down from DC. Mostly better, too, and real green instead of vape pens. He could calculate fractions and cost quicker than a math teacher. Aunt Tabby still called him a deadbeat. But Jackson made bank, and my aunt could fuck right off to sunny California. Why should he slave away at the chicken plant when he pulled down more from dealing? He only sold pot, and only to people over eighteen, part of his deal with Talitha. She scared the hell outta me. People went to her for help instead of a doctor, and they said she was a witch. She visited Mama sometimes. Once I got brave enough to ask why she grew.

"'Cause it keeps a kid from working a shit job," she told me, whip-quick and just as sure.

"Ain't no one in town gonna bust Talitha," Mama said. "She's respectable."

Talitha smacked her shoulder. "Don't you badmouth me, girl. I'm no kind of respectable."

Talitha was definitely a witch. Pretty too—she had real hips, a D-cup, and long, dark hair. Too old for me, but pretty anyway. When she started up with her husband, Mama and Aunt Tabby laughed. "Aren't those girls crying now?" Aunt Tabby said.

"What?" I asked, glancing up from my homework. I was a senior in high school then and determined to graduate, no matter how much work it took.

"Talitha used to run 'round with girls sometimes," Aunt Tabby told me. "Wonder if that hot guy of hers knows she saw Lacey

Gray 'fore she got married, and Miss High-and-Mighty Charlotte Lanier back when she was plain old Charlotte Price."

Mama turned from the stove, where she was adding frozen peppers to ramen. "Talitha never been serious 'bout anyone but that man she's got. She only saw girls on the side, and you know she only did 'cause she didn't want to deal with men."

Maybe she was never serious about those girls, I wanted to say. *Maybe she knew Lacey and Charlotte weren't right for her, or maybe she only wanted something casual.* Instead, I kept quiet. They asked me about guys sometimes. I lied.

I passed out cold after another long night. In the morning, I could shower the club's grossness off. Diamond slept like shit, one reason to wrap it up, and running water might wake her. She'd slam outta bed and stomp into the broken-locked bathroom, all dirty laundry and pink-mold tile.

If you got a respectable job, you wouldn't have to shower in the middle of the goddamn night, she'd shout, and the whole house would wake up to watch us argue.

I'd say, *You showered after every day of your respectable chicken-plant job, back before you got knocked up.*

Then Diamond would call me a tattooed whore. My mama, aunt, and brother would stand in the hall, silent. *Stop*, Jett would mouth, and I'd ignore him, feeling awful that he had to see it. I might have to storm out, 'cause you can't hit a pregnant girl, even if she is your sister. I'd have to call Alyssa and pray she'd pick up, then beg for a spot on her couch. Maybe one day, I could afford my own place. I saved everything I could, crossed my fingers, and hoped. It was hard. Mama didn't make me give her money, but she might as well have. Sighing loudly, she'd say, "How are we gonna afford groceries this week?" She wouldn't ask, not outright, but she'd give me a look, one loud as if she'd spoken. *I know you got money in your purse, Emmy Ann*, she'd be hinting, saying it without saying it at all.

So I'd hand her money. Mama kept a roof over our heads. What else could I do?

And I needed things. Not big ones, but little ones, and you'll die from a hundred cuts as sure as one big wound. I had to buy hair stuff, and snacks; I paid for my phone. I needed gas, and cigarettes, and I saved for my car insurance. Once in a while, I'd buy something I didn't need at all, something special, like a sparkly phone case or a box of fried chicken. Sometimes, you just break. Tired of saying no, no, no all the time, you need something in your life to say yes. Everyone snarks, "Well, you wouldn't be poor if..." and they'll tell you what you're doing wrong. Those people, they've never stood on the outside looking in. The whole world's a toy store, and you're the kid outside pressing your nose on the window.

I had to help Jett, too. Where was he 'sposed to get money for football fees, or phone minutes, or those dates he was starting to go on? Mama wouldn't give it to him. She'd say, *We can't afford that*, and one more time, he'd get left out, left behind. Kids are like any other herd animal; they'll tear at the weakest just to watch them bleed. When you're different, poor or shy or crooked-toothed, they'll go at you like a pack of feral hogs. You can't stop them—you can only offer up another victim. Pick at smaller, weaker kids, and the others will turn on them instead. It's survival, mostly. Playgrounds are a pretty feral place when you come right down to it. Jett needed all the help he could get.

So my move-out fund hardly existed. I tried my best. But poverty has a way of sucking you back. It's a whirlpool, always dragging you down, and you swim and swim just to keep your head above water. Only the strongest break out.

I was determined to be one of them.

AT NOON, I woke to a mostly empty house, Diamond snoring across the room. At least I had enough hot water. At least I had decent conditioner, deodorant, and a straightening iron. Thank God for small mercies. When you're as poor as the average Joiner, you learn to appreciate them.

Our kitchen window was small, and day craned to reach it. When I was little, I wished for a sunny morning kitchen, all honey-gold light. Afternoon drew breakfast's wreckage in dull grays. Dishes piled the stained countertop, and the faucet dripped like a cold nose. I shoved some utility bills aside and poured myself off-brand Rice Krispies. Diamond was still asleep, so I jammed my feet into a pair of old sneakers and slipped off down the swamp trail. If Mama and Aunt Tabby harassed me for dancing, they downright bitched about my walks. *You stay away from that swamp,* they'd say. *People walk in and don't walk out. You know so-and-so...* and they'd drone about that Carson kid vanishing or Ellis Rockland gone missing. Sometimes they'd get creative and rant about will o' the wisps that led to alligator-filled streams, or crows that spoke in human voices. All ridiculous. Everyone knew Beau Carson's brother killed him, and Ellis Rockland disappeared almost two decades before. The rest of it was superstitious bullshit.

I'd been escaping to the swamp since we moved in about five years before. Every time I walked under that green-leaf canopy, I waited, almost hoped, that something weird would happen. It never did. The swamp's green faded to gray in the long distance, and Spanish moss tangled like a sleeping woman's hair. The swamp seemed to have—I'd struggled to find the right word—a presence all its own. Something watched and waited there. Why did it scare everyone? The world would hurt you. The woods went about their own business. In the swamp, I didn't have to pretend I enjoyed giving those lap dances, not like at the club, where I smiled like a kid on school picture day, all the time thinking, *I like women, you worthless bastard, and even if I did guys, I wouldn't touch you.* Instead, I walked for miles. I could shed Emmy the stripper and become Emerald, jewel-bright and finally alive.

About forty minutes into the swamp, I found my favorite place, where a pretty stream curved around an enormous cypress. I settled into a mossy spot tucked between its knees. The world smelled like honeysuckle and growing things. No one would call me a useless Joiner there. No one would offer me money for sex. Zeke's words still stung: *You'll fuck them McAllister boys but not me?* So what if I'd lost it with Alyssa's cousin Whit, back when I was fifteen? But the sheriff caught us at the Lot in the back of Whit's pickup, and he raised holy hell. Whit got threatened with statutory, not 'cause I didn't consent—the whole town knew we'd been going out for six months—but 'cause that sheriff knew he could do it. If I was a rich-ass Lanier girl and Whit was a Nesmith boy, Nash Briggs would've driven on by. The less you got, the more they come after you. Ask me how I know.

Not that I particularly loved Whit or something. It seemed like time to lose it, so I did. I'd have rather been with a girl, but they were untouchable as the moon. Guys were easier, even if they smelled musky and waved their dicks around like little boys with play swords. A girl would've been better. A girl would smell pretty, like fancy mall soap, and we could've shared clothes and makeup, laughing in that sleepy quiet before breakfast. Another girl would never have called me a slut 'cause I danced. *You do what you have to*, she'd say, 'cause she understood—maybe she'd have to do it too, like Alyssa. *We know what you really like.*

"What are you doing out here all alone?" someone said into the swamp's deep quiet, and I startled so hard I almost fell in the creek. A girl with green eyes stood on the trail, a beautiful girl, all long legs and long, black hair—I liked long hair too, but I didn't think about pulling it. Tattooed vines climbed from her coppery ankles to her thighs, from her wrists to her shoulders. Their stems tangled and forked; I didn't recognize the plant, but her artist was very, very good.

"I asked what you were doing out here all alone," the girl said. She was smiling.

"I'm just—I go for walks," I replied, hating myself, 'cause of course I sounded stupid. I wasn't used to talking to beautiful girls, or beautiful anyone, really. Lower Congaree was a little short on beauty, and maybe that was the real reason I hiked into the swamp.

"I'm Zara. Zara Fenwick." She plopped down next to me like she'd been invited. Close enough that we were already friends, maybe. I'd never met anyone in that deep, cool forest, much less a pretty girl. "Who're you?"

I hesitated. Everywhere else I was Emmy the wild child, Emmy the stripper, Emmy the useless white trash. I inhaled that rich, ripe scent of fertile dirt. That smell meant safety. "I'm Emerald," I told her, and sat up straight, shoulders back, like Mama taught. Not that I wanted to think about Mama. I didn't want to think about any of them.

"You sure about that, Emerald?" Her shiny hair and perfect teeth seemed a world away from Lower Congaree. A brown dress rucked high on her thighs.

All around us, the swamp sang insect drone and birdsong, treefrog hymns and woodpecker taps. "Yeah," I said. "I'm sure. What're you doing here?"

"I asked you first, and you obviously walked in here so you didn't give me a good answer." She kept smiling. My heart thumped, partly from the scare and partly 'cause she was gorgeous.

"I was hiking. There's a path behind my house." I didn't say "trailer" and I didn't add "I share it with my mom and aunt," 'cause Zara had tattooed vines twining her calves and eyes like summer sunshine. She looked my age, but I didn't dare hope.

"I live around here." Zara flicked her hand like the queen of some familiar country. On the edge of town, then, like me. People like the Joiners, we didn't live in the middle of anything. We were the kind of people who clung to the world's weedy margins. "I never see anyone out here," she said. "Tell me everything about you, Emerald."

She must've been as lonely as me. Small towns are a special kind of lonesome. You know everyone and everyone knows you, but they stick you in a box and say, "This is so-and-so, and she's like this." Then they never change their mind. If you do something horrible, like kill a person or hurt a kid, then they say, "Well, I always thought she was like that. I could see it in her," like they have to be right, even in hindsight. Like they have to know you, even if they didn't, all along. I wondered if Zara saw that same sadness in me, right away, without even asking.

She was waiting. Zara sat with her elbow on her thigh and her chin in her hand, the perfect thinker, like that statue. Far away, crows called.

I might as well begin at the beginning. "I was born here in Lower Congaree—"

"No, no, no." Zara emphasized each word. "Lower Congaree is out there. This is the Congaree Swamp. Anyway. Keep going."

"So I was born in Lower Congaree?" I said it like a question, like I wasn't sure. I wanted to get everything right. "I've lived there all my life—I mean, we moved around a lot, but we stayed in town? I graduated from Congaree High School—"

"Oh, poor you." Zara swooped me into a sudden hug. Her dark hair smelled like honeysuckle and broken leaves. "That's so awful. They're terrible there, aren't they? And you couldn't tell anyone you liked girls because they'd hurt you."

I leapt up. "I'm sorry, I have to go." No one knew my secret. The swamp was safe. How could she tell?

"You don't have to go." Zara tugged me down again. "Stop freaking out and keep telling me about you. It's different here. What do you do all day?"

The sun stretched long, pale fingers through the trees, and wind whispered in the branches. If I listened hard enough, it would tell me stories I was never meant to know. The swamp *was* different. There, no one called me names or offered me money to fuck. Mama didn't shout about my job. I wasn't Emmy Joiner, shoved into a neat little box and scared of the whole wide world. "I don't know," I said. "I sleep late and—read, watch TV, mess around on my phone, I guess. I, uh, work at night." I had to say it and what would Zara think? "I dance. I mean, at work. That's what I do. You know, exotic dancing."

"Oooh." Maybe Zara was looking at me. Staring at the trees, I couldn't stand to peek. "I bet guys like that. I bet you're good at it, too. You're so pretty."

I almost sagged onto the moss with relief. "Uh, thanks. I was scared—I worried you'd think—I don't know. You know what people think about dancers."

"It's so stupid." Zara's laugh fit with the birdsong and rustling leaves. "If you're pretty, why shouldn't people look? I want to see you dance sometime. Tell me more, Emerald."

When she used my real name again, something hurt inside me uncurled. Zara knew I was a bisexual stripper, and she called me Emerald. She hadn't run away. So I told her about living with my mama and aunt, and about Diamond bitching, and Jett skipping school. "They call us trailer trash," I said. "Guys always think I'm a prostitute 'cause I'm a broke-ass Joiner, and what wouldn't we do for money?" I wanted to slump against that cypress tree and close my eyes. Just thinking about it, that loneliness flooded me again, like no one knew me and no one ever would. "They're awful. We can't catch a break, you know? And if they knew I was bi they'd lose it. It's bad enough that I dance. If they knew I liked girls—"

"They're horrible." When I dared to glance at Zara, she was watching me. "I hate them, too."

"I could've gone to college." My throat went tight, like I'd swallowed a marble. "I mean, maybe. If I tried harder. Mama said college was a waste of time and money, so I didn't bother." She also said college was for rich kids and we were poor as dirt. I didn't want to tell Zara that. I didn't want to say that girls like me didn't go to college, even if we dreamed of it, 'cause we didn't fit in. Looking down their noses at me, those pretty rich girls would say things like, *Where are you from again?* and *What did you say your parents do?* Decent people have married parents, or at least divorced ones. Having kids without a man attached is trashy, and respectable daddies don't skip town.

"They're wrong about you. You deserve better than they treat you, Emerald." Zara picked up my wrist. When she traced the flower there, I went very still. She tucked her chin like a Disney deer. "I like your rose," she told me. "Do you have any more?"

My palmetto and crescent moon had taken six sessions, and I couldn't miss the chance to show it off, especially to another girl with ink. I'd saved for a year to get that tattoo. All my anger and sadness seemed to lift up and float away. I turned and pulled my tank a little lower. "It goes all the way down my back," I said.

"Let me see."

Was she flirting? Was this how one girl told another, *I like girls too, and I like you in particular?* But I took my clothes off every night, so I yanked my shirt up to my neck.

Soft fingers trailed over my spine, and I shivered like someone had dripped cold water on my back. People touched me all the time, but not like that. They groped and pawed, even Whit— maybe especially Whit, and Mel Heyward, and all those other guys. I wasn't a whore like they said, but I didn't stay Mother-Mary-pure, either.

"This is really beautiful," Zara told me.

"I like yours, too," I said.

"Thanks." She stretched out her arm, like she was examining them herself. "I like them a lot. They turned out well, don't you think?"

The next step baffled me. Did it always go so quick? I didn't know the dance steps.

"You're so pretty," she told me. "I haven't seen such a pretty girl in a long time." *Me either*, I could've said, but I didn't. I couldn't talk. My skin goosebumped under her touch. "I think I want to kiss you."

"Excuse me?" Wind murmured high in the tupelo trees; the insect whir and birdsong sunk to a strange quiet. "Uh, we're moving really fast—"

"That doesn't matter. I feel like I know you already. Do you want to kiss?" Zara's fingers drifted over me, all the better for their tickly-light dawdling. A gorgeous girl was stroking my back, and it couldn't be that different from kissing a guy, not really. I'd done plenty of that. So I shimmied my shirt down and faced her. If she wanted it so bad she could make the first move, I told myself. Really, I was too scared to do it myself.

"So pretty," Zara said. She rose to her knees and kissed me. Her lips were softer than any guy's, soft as the snowflakes I'd never seen, not in real life. Zara pulled me close and her pretty breasts pressed mine. I dared to slip my tongue past those pouty lips. I'd have done anything for lips like hers.

When her gentle fingers found my nipple, my breath caught. She played with it, then pulled back and pinched. Desire tap-danced low in my belly. "D'you like that?" she asked, like she couldn't tell. "You're fun."

Couldn't I touch her if she touched me first? I cupped her

breast. She didn't stop me so I thumbed her nipple, and it tightened to a wicked eyeful under her thin dress.

"Like that," Zara said. When she kissed me again, her teeth nipped my lip. I'd wanted a girl's warm curves for so long, and this pretty stranger seemed unbelievable, like a spell or an answered prayer. She drew me nearer and her finger slipped between my cheeks. No one had ever touched me there, not ever, and its gleaming newness caught my breath.

Then she stopped.

I made my eyes wide and begging, a kid asking for one more piece of candy.

"Nope." Zara tapped my nose like you'd bop a disobedient puppy. "That's enough. You can meet me here again tomorrow. Same time."

"But—"

She popped to her feet. "Tomorrow. See you tomorrow."

I couldn't let her run away so fast. Had I done something wrong? I must not have, 'cause she wanted to see me again, but I couldn't help thinking it anyway. "We just started—"

Zara was already striding down the trail.

Want simmered as I tramped home. I slipped against myself and that want soared into need. My black undies soaked through. Mama and Aunt Tabby were at work. Maybe—but when I slid in my bedroom door, face flushed, Diamond was still snoring. Goddammit. I couldn't even get myself off in peace. My whole body hummed and there was nothing to do about it. After I pulled off my cutoffs, I flopped into bed. Diamond had to fuck around and get knocked up. I had to be poor enough to share a room. I closed my eyes and wished for somewhere else. But mostly, I wished for Zara.

I woke up sometime around four. Work started at seven, so I spent an hour straightening my hair and doing my makeup, then wandered to the kitchen for dinner. I always got dressed at the club, even if the backstage room skeeved me out, 'cause Mama raised holy hell if she saw my clothes. *You look like that Britney Spears video*, she'd say, flipping at my plaid skirt. I wouldn't know what she meant, but I'd keep my face blank and my mouth shut. A long time ago, I learned to treat her harassment like a person might treat a hurricane: You can't stop it; you can only nail up the shutters and pray. Mama was real big on respect. You didn't talk back, and you sure as hell didn't tell her no. You just took whatever she doled out, nodded your head and waited for it to end. *Always walking outta here looking like a whore. It's one thing to be one and another to look like it. D'you know what people think of our family 'cause of you?* On and on. It'd only make me angry, bottled-up anger that eventually would explode and hurt everyone in its way. I'd dress later.

Jett was scribbling at summer school homework on the kitchen table. He'd flunk sophomore year if he didn't pass, and Mama would belt the hell outta him. *Why can't none of you kids work hard?* she'd shout. He might've been too old to cry, but he'd cry anyway. "Hey, Emmy," he said.

"Hey, Emmy baby," Mama called from the stove. Her back bent, and her shoulders slouched. Gray hair rooted behind her fake red. It made her look much older than forty-two. After a long day of work, she didn't have enough energy to dye her hair. I didn't blame her. "Jett, you get on that homework."

"Yes, ma'am," he muttered, and dropped his head again.

"Whatcha making?" I asked as I slid into a chair.

She hadn't turned around yet, but she would. Then the shouting might start. "Ramen with vegetables again."

We ate a lot of ramen. Mama dropped frozen veggies in it, but they couldn't disguise that miserable fake-chicken taste. You want to taste poverty, eat a pack of ramen or some Kraft mac and cheese —not Velveeta. You need bling to afford pre-made cheese sauce.

"How was work?" I asked. Me and Mama didn't have much to talk about; I had my life and she had hers. No one called her a whore, but she plucked feathers off dead chickens. You make compromises in the world, trade one flavor of bad for another. I've seen it too many times.

"Work was work," Mama said, which meant no better or worse than any other day.

Tummy first, Diamond waddled in. She was fit to bust but somehow hanging on. She'd wanted an abortion, but they killed Roe versus Wade and you couldn't get an appointment. Out-of-staters were crowding South Carolina abortion clinics. They'd probably outlaw it for good soon—one more reason to steer clear of guys.

"How was the swamp, Emmy?" my sister asked, 'cause she liked to start shit.

Mama whirled from the stove. "How many times have I told you not to go out there, goddammit!" she snapped. Jett winced and ducked lower, like he could escape as long as he hunched up small. "D'you know how many people disappeared back there? You might dress like a hooker at work, but we don't want nothing to happen to you!"

Of course she dragged my clothes into it. I sagged into a chair and waited for the storm tide to break. I was stupid, irresponsible, and didn't have the brains God gave a goose. I was about as sharp as a marble, and it was gonna be the death of me. Our kitchen was small, cramped with our table crammed in, and Mama's anger sucked up any room we had left. I focused on the scarred wall. There was the patched hole repaired before we moved in; its height and placement said someone punched it in. There was the grease stain from Aunt Tabby throwing spaghetti at Jackson, and a ghost of green body paint, made when Diamond's Halloween costume brushed a corner. Odd black marks curled like runaway punctuation. Someone should've stopped to scrub them, but no one had time or inclination.

Of course, smack in the middle of the shouting, Talitha Merle walked in. Maybe she'd knocked. Mama was yelling too loud to hear.

"What's this about?" Talitha asked. All that dark hair spilled down her shoulders, and I wished one more time that she wasn't so old or so married, and maybe didn't scare me half to death.

"Emmy wandered into the swamp again today!" Mama said. "We told her over and over, and she still walks on back there like she owns the thing. You talk some sense into her, Talitha. Don't nobody know that place like you."

Talitha sat across from me. She smelled like lavender and I tried not to think about it. "There's things in that swamp you never wanna see," she said, and her voice was low and serious, a teacher telling me I'd best buckle down and work or else. "Don't you go back there. You might not come out again, and you don't wanna know how I know that."

"Maybe I do," I said, 'cause I didn't have anything to lose. I'd already lost most things worth having, or I never had them in the first place. Our kitchen went very still then, the quiet that comes before a thunderstorm. Aunt Tabby had snuck in—the whole family was watching me get yelled at. We only had basic cable, and I guess it was better than TV.

"My own daddy disappeared into that swamp," Talitha told me. "He never came out again." Her steady, solemn voice told me she wasn't lying, either. I knew truth when I heard it.

"That what happened to him?" Mama asked.

"You don't go in that swamp," Talitha said, Mama's words passing like a breeze. "You hear me, Emmy? You'll regret it. You disappear, the sheriff won't go look more than two hundred yards into that muck. I know Nash Briggs, and he's smart enough to be scared."

I watched my hands. They were small and pale, my fingernails black as a goth girl's. "What if there are people back there?" I asked.

"There's nobody you wanna meet." Talitha still spoke in that serious, come-to-Jesus, get-your-life-straight voice. "People go in there, they come back changed. Like I said, nobody knows that more than me." She stood up, and a heaviness lifted. Just like that, the conversation was over. "I didn't mean to come during dinnertime," she told Mama. "I'll leave y'all be."

"No, no, sit down," Mama said, like I knew she would. We didn't have much but Mama never let anyone walk away from our table. So Talitha sat, and they ran through the usual Lower Congaree gossip—who got married, who got pregnant, who got thrown in jail. After about ten minutes, I said, "Well, gotta get to work, y'all," even though I didn't have to be there for another hour, and I'd miss dinner besides. Whatever. I could grab some fries at the club.

"Bye," Jett said, still hunched up. Mama scared the hell outta him.

"You remember what I said, Emmy Joiner," Talitha told me.

"Yes, ma'am," I replied, and I sort of meant it and sort of didn't. Luckily my car started again, and I fought with myself as I drove those dinky backroads, then the broad swamp highway. Everyone in town agreed that if Talitha Merle gave you advice, she was as serious as a heart attack and twice as urgent. But Zara had kissed me. She'd called me Emerald, and her skin was soft as satin. I didn't want to give her up on Talitha Merle's say-so.

Drainage ditches lined both sides of the road; people said sleek-fat catfish swam in them. They said those fish would gobble you down to bare bones. I wasn't sure if I believed it, but I sure as hell didn't care to learn the truth. Talitha and Mama were sorta right. You didn't fuck with the swamp. People in Lower Congaree recited that like one of God's own commandments, and if I hadn't been going back there for so many years, I'd have been scared, too. But I never saw anything strange in the swamp, not once, not even a will o' the wisp. I had to decide who to listen to, those tired women or my own yearning need. I couldn't make up my mind. Sometimes you just pick your poison and pray.

Sunset was still an hour off when I pulled into the Bottoms Up parking lot. I hated coming to work in the daylight. It felt grimy and strange, like fingernail dirt that won't wash out, no matter how hard you scrub. The club's outside looked dingy, sad, all black walls and cigarette butts mashed in the dirt. Some greaseball guys were hanging near the front door. Not smoking, not talking, just standing there like they had nothing better to do. I walked past with my eyes down, but I felt them staring.

Like usual, Noah was behind the bar. His daddy owned the place, and he was more proud of that than he should've been, but I liked him anyway. Between his puppy-dog eyes and messy hair, I tended to forget how big he was. Like a lot of guys in Lower Congaree, Noah spent his spare time doing bench presses, mostly 'cause there wasn't shit else to do. "Hey, girl," he said. "How you doing tonight?"

"I'm doing," I replied. *I kissed a girl*, I could've said. *Or rather, she kissed me. It was everything I hoped for. But Mama says I can't go into the swamp again, so I can't see her, and that's as bad as the kiss was good.* "Y'all calling in an order soon?" I asked instead. Bottoms Up had to serve food to serve liquor, so they sent out to The Roadhouse, a mile up the road. Noah's daddy Kurt owned that, too.

"Pretty soon, probably," Noah told me. "You want something?"

"Just some fries," I said.

"You want a drink before you get changed?" he asked.

Some girls got drunk before work—Noah would give two drinks on the house, strong ones, and more at a discount. He said it made the girls better dancers, and it did, mostly 'cause they stopped caring what people thought. They also stopped noticing where people put their hands.

"I'm good," I told him, like I said every night, and slid through the crowd to the dressing room. Bentley was already shaking what God gave her, and we had about twenty guys scattered around, most drooling over her and eating chicken wings—Thursday was twenty wings for fifteen bucks. Noah said his daddy lost money on the wings but made it up in drinks.

"Hey, Luna," said Savannah, half outta her clothes already. Everyone in town knew I was Emmy Joiner, but I had to pick a stage name—we all had them—so I picked Luna 'cause it sounded kinda gothy, with the moon and all. I dressed gothy, too, wore black undies and black nail polish. I'd have worn halters and collars and chains too, if I had enough courage. Guys like goth girls. They think we're more likely to do freaky stuff, and any guy who tells you he doesn't want that is lying. They like you on your knees, and if they don't, it's 'cause they want to be on their knees instead. Dance for six months and you'll know it's true.

I thought about that, and about picking a new name and why I did it. I wanted to tell Zara. *I can't even be myself at that club*, I'd say, then I remembered that I might not see her again. Sadness dropped like a sick weight. I had to decide if I'd listen to Mama or go my own way, and Mama could make me listen. She'd tear my life into misery with shouting arguments, and it was easier sometimes, quicker, to duck my head and say, "Yes, ma'am." People will tell you to follow your heart, but it can be like struggling to swim when you're tied to an anchor. Sometimes the battle isn't worth it. They'll drown you in the end.

I shoved it away. Best not to dwell on disappointment, and I had to smile, smile, smile. I'd be sad after work. Just then, I needed to hustle. *You're Luna*, I told myself as I stripped to my black thong. *You like guys, and they like you back.* Wiggling, I wrangled on my garter belt, stockings, bra top, and high heels. I knew Luna real well by then. She was quieter than the other dancers, a good listener, sort of brainless and giggly. Guys loved her.

The night wore on like any other. The club was a kind of church, one where men came to worship bodies instead of God. Not women—they didn't particularly like women, and most of them had women at home, anyway. They wanted to get away from their women. "She doesn't love me anymore," they'd say when they got drunk enough. "I stay around for the kids. If I leave, I'll never see 'em again." Those were the nice guys. Others would tell you that their woman let herself go, which generally meant she had a baby. "Well, who put that baby there?" I'd want to ask. Some guys would outright tell you their wife was a bitch. "She treats me like shit," they'd say, and you'd know there was another side to that story.

You'd think they came in 'cause they were horny. Most were, but horniness will only get you in the door. Those guys stuck around to play make-believe. Whether or not they whipped it out, they wanted to pretend they were Hugh Hefner. These were broke-ass men who worked all day at a chicken plant or lumber company or lawn care service, places that paid them minimum wage to shut up and take whatever their bosses handed them. They wore dirty jeans; they smelled like sweat and cigarette smoke. The type of guy who came into the club, he didn't have much to offer, or he didn't think he did. So he paid us to play king for a day, and we made him feel sexy, wanted. We gave him what real life promised and snatched back—call it control, or love, or a sense of self-worth. We traded in lost fantasies and fairy tales. Remember that next time you see a club. They call us sex workers, but we aren't, not really. We don't sell sex. We hand out dreams.

Caught on mirrored walls, our reflections went on and on, a miniature infinity; sometimes I liked to think about that and sometimes I didn't. Hard-edged but somehow vague, the club always seemed stuck in a hazy hour between midnight and one, and after a while, you felt the backbeat in your fingertips. Everything smelled like sex and cigarettes—it's illegal to smoke inside, but when the sheriff's deputies were sucking down Marlboro Reds, no one gave a fuck. Recirculated air dried your mouth, and people drank too much. Even me, sucking down plain Cokes, my glass rim would go sticky with lip gloss, and I'd remind myself not to chew ice.

We were black-lit and beautiful in it. When our DJ played the first scraping notes of "Closer," I stepped onstage. Every time, I did the same dance, hardly a dance at all. Bright stage lights drew the men as a dark, faceless crowd. I focused on that anonymous dark and moved the way they liked, all slinky grace. They slid money in my thong. I shook my ass. They wanted me, and I wished they were girls. After two songs, my back hurt and my feet ached. I was working the tables when, like every night, one of the guys called me Emmy.

"I'm Luna here, baby," I told him, all fake smiles while my stomach pitched. When I sat in his lap, he grabbed my side. I managed not to cringe. Tuck, our bouncer, only stopped guys who pawed what he called our "bathing suit areas."

"How much d'you charge to go out back?" the guy whispered.

"I don't do that, honey." I laughed like he'd said something funny.

I almost recognized his weak eyes and dull hair; maybe he was one of those Wheeler guys. Reverend Jack Wheeler, who preached at the Holiness church, he had about a dozen dirty-faced kids. Trust the preacher's son to show up at a strip club. "I got a hundred bucks here that says you do more than dance," the guy told me.

"I'd cost a lot more than that." I smiled again. A strip club will teach you to smile at terrible things if you didn't already know how. Me, I learned real small. I learned to smile when Mama didn't have much money for Christmas, and when boys at school looked up my skirt; when Mama made ramen for the fourth night in a row and teachers glanced down my tank top. If your Thanksgiving turkey comes from the food pantry, the world teaches you to tolerate a lot.

"Two hundred," the guy said, and he raised his voice to make sure I heard.

I shook my head again, and that smile never moved. I could've been Miss America.

"I can do two fifty but no more," he told me.

I wanted to say, *If you ask me that one more time, I'll get the bouncer to kick your ass out, and he might take that phrase literally. I don't like guys, not ones like you.* Instead I giggled and focused on my toes. "You're really cute, but I can't. I'm a good girl." They liked to hear that, and his arm tightened around my waist. He wasn't cute at all.

The guy settled on a thirty-dollar lap dance. He'd really thought I'd fuck him for a little more than the price of three of them. Some of the girls might've done it, or at least held out for three hundred. Elecktra probably would've. She worked every night 'cause she wanted her kids to have Barbie Dream Houses and soccer gear. I hoped those kids loved her. I hoped they didn't know how their mama got money for a Nintendo Switch.

I shimmied through the low light and cigarette smoke. Elektra was doing her best by her babies, and it shouldn't've mattered what she did. *Nothing sadder than a C-section scar on a stripper*, a guy said once, and I balled my fist but kept smiling. He didn't know a goddamn thing, not one. I thought about that guy while I danced—the light drawing his face in sharp, mean angles, the smirk twisting his mouth. I pushed my tits in the Wheeler kid's face and thought about how you did the best you could with what you had. I made more money than Mama and Aunt Tabby. I made more money than Jackson. I was saving up for my own place, and every dancer says it but I was saving up for an education, too. Not college but some kinda school, cooking or massage or cosmetology. Anything that wouldn't see me breaking my back in a chicken plant. So I played with my tits, and I rubbed against that guy, and I hoped he kept his hands planted on the arms of that chair.

Finally, the dance ended. They always do. Someone said once that as long as you hold your breath, you can do anything for ten minutes. Maybe they were right. I took my cash and grabbed my fries from the bar. I could've carried them back to the dressing room, but it was ick, and my eyes would've got accustomed to the brighter light.

I ate. I used the dancer's bathroom. I fended off requests for a private room—guys liked to get the girls back there and ask for sex. When they played Marilyn Manson's "Tainted Love," I stepped onto that strange altar and took my clothes off again. I imagined the hooting men were pretty girls, and I smiled. I wished the men watching me were Zara. I'd probably never see her again. I tried not to think about that. I tried not to think about her sunshine eyes and her soft lips on mine. She'd kissed me like I was special, like we had time and time and time.

We closed around four on Thursday nights. Sometimes that felt like nine at night and sometimes it felt like noon—you lose track. I was giggling with an old guy when Noah yelled for last call, and that Wheeler kid slipped up behind me. "I can do three hundred," he said into my ear. I could've reeled away from his booze-breath.

I made myself laugh. "I told you, I'm a good girl."

The old guy paid his bar tab and handed me an extra twenty. Old guys are usually good that way. They're grateful for someone who makes them feel young again. It's a sad kind of magic, but the best girls can do it without trying. I kissed his cheek and ducked out to the dressing room before the customers left and the lights went up. The club's a special kind of sad in the light, all empty glasses and spilled drinks, like a daydream gone stale. I didn't want to see it. After I changed, I stood at the door and waited for Noah to take me to my car. He won't let dancers walk through a dark parking lot alone.

"Hey, three fifty." The Wheeler boy ducked out of the shadows as I leapt and clutched my chest.

"You scared me!" I scolded cutely.

"I'm serious, three fifty." He smelled like cheap cigarettes and cheaper beer. I almost retched. "You know you'll do it for that much."

And maybe it was tempting. I'd probably pulled three hundred that night, not bad for Thursday, but three hundred and fifty was almost a third of our rent. For the teeniest sliver of a moment, I saw Mama's gray part and creased forehead, a pen tapping her lips as she scribbled numbers on envelopes. But she'd've said, *Where'd all this money come from, Emmy Ann?* I'd never crossed that line, not once. I didn't want to make their rumors true. Even if I did, I'd have hated every second.

"I told you, I don't do that." I smiled again. I had to.

He reached for my wrist, and that half-breath felt like falling down a long, dark well.

"Leave her the fuck alone!" There was Noah, shoving him back. "Don't you fucking touch her, y'hear me? Get outta here before I call the sheriff and your dad in that order, you fucking Jesus freak."

He was definitely a Wheeler, then. His daddy might've kicked his ass all the way to Sunday morning if he got caught at the club.

He wobbled for a second, spun, then almost fell. Then he spit at Noah's feet and staggered into the still, hot night.

"Sorry, Luna." Noah took my arm. "You shouldn't have to put up with that shit. It's 'cause you're pretty." He gave me one of those what-can-you-do-about-it smiles. "Lemme walk you to your car. We'll wait til he leaves, okay?"

I didn't get outta there til four-thirty, and Mama's alarm was blaring by the time I hit my bed. Diamond snored through it. On account of being so sick, she didn't have to work. She'd have slept with that Wheeler guy and kept the cash for herself. *Dress like a whore and you'll get treated like one*, Mama always told me.

I hated that she was right.

Your first thought of the day is important. My gramma always said that. She didn't mean the everyday "I have to pee," or "My alarm's going off." She meant that first deliberate thought, the one that cuts through your morning static. On Friday, I thought of Zara. *Tomorrow*, she'd told me. *I'll see you tomorrow.*

She wouldn't, I decided. Talitha had been telling the truth, and I ought not to walk back into that swamp, no matter how much I liked Zara. Goddammit. I'd finally met a girl, and I couldn't see her again. Maybe I'd run into her in town, at the Gas N Go or McAllister's grocery store. I could hope. Strange I'd never seen her before—Lower Congaree was so small. Maybe she'd just moved in, or maybe she kept to herself. Diamond was still snoring, so I slipped into the bathroom. When I finished my shower, I dressed and wandered into the kitchen.

It was a lazy summer morning, and the trees had gone the dark, tired green that comes in August's deepest dog days. It hadn't rained in two weeks. The grass was baked brown, and even the weeds had crisped. Our window units hummed endlessly, tunelessly, trying to keep up with the hundred-degree heat. I was settling breakfast when Diamond walked into the kitchen. She grabbed a banana, and we sat at the table together, two people in one house without much to say to each other.

"How d'you feel this morning?" I finally asked.

"Like shit," she replied around her banana. "I wish this baby would hurry up and come already."

She had three more months. She probably didn't want to think about it. I wouldn't, if I were her.

"You know, you oughta listen to Mama," she said.

"About what?" I asked. Mama harassed me about so many things, and Diamond could've meant any of them. Crispy Rice clumped my mouth. I'd hear it from her, whatever it was.

"About work. You can get a good job—"

My spoon splatted my milk. "I make good money, and it's not the chicken plant."

Her eyes went piggy and mean, and I knew we'd skip through the same argument then. The words changed, but its tune stayed the same. "What, you too good to work there? You think your shit don't stink? You don't take your clothes off to work in the chicken plant, and you don't fuck the chickens."

I sagged into my chair. "You gonna talk like that when your baby gets here?"

"Maybe not," she said. "Mama always talked like that in front of you, and look how you turned out."

I stared at my Crispy Rice, already going soggy. I wasn't gonna eat it. Aunt Tabby would've harassed me for wasting food, but everything tastes bad when you're miserable, no matter how hungry you are. "I wish, just for once, that I could have an actual conversation with someone in this house," I said, mostly to myself, 'cause my sister didn't care. "Every time I try and talk, it's all 'Your clothes are awful' or 'Your job is awful' or 'Don't do this or that.' No one cares how I feel about any of it."

"Yeah, 'cause you're wrong," Diamond said, mouth still full. "If someone hurts you at work, it'll be your fault." She grabbed another banana. I dumped my bowl into the sink. Normally I'd have drank the milk, but I couldn't stomach it. Diamond really believed that old lie. *Well, she asked for it*, people would say. The rest of my family probably agreed.

Pieces fell into place then, like I'd dumped a bucket of blocks and formed a perfect tower. My job and clothes made me fair game. If someone grabbed me or jumped me in the parking lot, they'd say, *Well, he wouldn't have done it if...* then rant about my clothes or my job. *Emmy Ann, you brought this on yourself*, Mama would tell me. Aunt Tabby and Diamond would nod along with her.

No one fought for me, not ever. The worst things could happen. I could get beaten, raped, murdered. I could disappear. They still wouldn't fight.

I balled my fist. I could've punched a hole in the wall then, jammed knuckles and broken bones on that cheap drywall. Crying, I'd have cradled that hand and slid to the floor. I'd have sobbed from the pain, and I'd have sobbed with the betrayal. They thought I deserved it. I couldn't decide which I wanted more, the smashing or the sobbing. If I stayed, I'd give in to one or the other, then Diamond would tattle to Mama and I'd get it twice. *Well your sister was right*, she'd say. It would've sucked the wind outta me, like a sucker punch you never saw coming. I had to get out. Zara would understand. Just then, I didn't care if the Lord Jesus Christ had come down from heaven and told me to stay away from that swamp. Someone understood. I only had to walk in and find her.

Diamond would blab to Mama. She'd always been a big mouth, that kid who ran to tell who hit who or piped up to say so-

and-so's lying. Diamond could holler all the way to hell, 'cause I might've been a dancer but no one knocked me up. One lasts a hell of a lot longer than the other. Her baby daddy wasn't gonna help her, either—Brant Wilcox was just as poor as us, and pissed at her besides. He said that baby was her choice and her fault, like his dick had nothing to do with it. They hadn't spoken in two months. That baby would be born poor, and like every other Joiner, she'd die poor, too.

I fumed about all that as I stalked through the swamp. Diamond was one of those people who couldn't be unhappy on her own—she had to spread it around, like a bad cold. Her baby would come up in that. She'd either learn to dish it out or get quiet and take it.

Eventually I calmed down and started to notice the world again. A beamed ceiling of tree branches wove overhead, and every shade of green was different, each one new. Mud clotted the low places; birds sang like a Sunday choir. I wished I knew their names. Under the tall, green cypresses, the temperature dropped at least twenty degrees. Humidity clung like my mother never had, like the swamp's warm breath.

I could picture it then, the whole swamp spreading around me, all those trees and creeks and snarled green vines. If you looked, if you paid attention, you could see a whole world blooming. Birds sheltered in the trees; small creatures tucked themselves into the brush. Fish and frogs hid in deep-running creeks. Life seemed brand-new there, and maybe it was. Maybe we all came from the swamp, I thought. Maybe everything started in a place like this, where water met land and married in a glorious mud-puddle confusion.

When I rounded the corner to my favorite spot, Zara leapt from the moss. "You came!" she said, throwing her arms around me, and I realized I'd been so angry about Diamond I forgot to be nervous. Zara wore a short green dress, fraying on its edges. It was thin and I tried not to think about that. Instead, I concentrated on the smell of her hair, like honeysuckle in the rain.

"I worried you wouldn't come," she said, pulling me down to the moss. "Now, sit down and tell me everything."

"Before I do, where d'you live?" I asked. "My mama gets mad about me coming out in the swamp—"

Zara's laughter bubbled like a clear, bright stream. "There's nothing for you to be worried about back here."

"Mama and this friend of hers said it's dangerous." I phrased it carefully: *dangerous*. Under that tangly green canopy, among the golden flowers, I couldn't stand to accuse the forest. It held us in its kind, cupped hands. Trees murmured in the high-up wind, and the little creek babbled. It seemed to speak words I'd known once and forgotten. I could've curled up on that moss and slept.

Zara rearranged her long legs. Her tattooed vines were knotty, wild. I imagined tracing their stems right up her thighs. "Maybe it's dangerous if you think it's dangerous. Or maybe people just don't like it. Think about the word 'swamp.' It's so ugly. Why would you give this place such an ugly word?"

I'd never thought of that. It *was* an ugly word, short and squat, with a sound like spitting. "It seems terrible, doesn't it?" I said. "I've never seen anything strange back here, not once. But Mama said people disappear—"

"People can't *disappear*, Emerald." Zara petted the moss like it was a kitten, back and forth, back and forth. "Maybe they get lost, or go somewhere better, but they don't vanish into thin air."

"I guess not," I said. She was right. It sounded ridiculous.

"So tell me what you've been up to." She picked up my hand again, and her fingers tickled my wrist. "I want to hear everything."

So I told her about work, about that Wheeler boy, about Diamond and the terrible things she'd said. Zara's mouth puckered, and her brow drew down. The longer I spoke, the madder she looked. It felt good to see my anger written on someone else's face. "That's *horrible*," she said. "Like it's better to work at that awful plant. At least you aren't killing anything. I'm glad you came out here. You need to get away from all that."

"Thank you." I focused not on her face, but those vines circling her arms.

"They're awful," she told me. "Really, you shouldn't have to put up with them."

I wanted to run from that subject, run and never look back. The forest cradled us like its favorite secret. Maybe we were. I could've believed it. *It loves us*, I thought, then, *Don't be stupid. Forests can't love people.*

"Tell me about you," I said.

"I told you the other day. There isn't much to tell. I don't know. I like to watch birds and swim and hike." She flipped my wrist. "I really do like your rose, Emerald."

I wanted her to say my name over and over. "I love your tats, too." I was about to ask Zara if she liked movies when she raised my wrist to her lips and kissed its sensitive underside. Without meaning to, I shivered.

"I think I should kiss you again." Her eyes caught and held mine. She saw me and she didn't flinch, or make a face, or say, *Well Emmy, you know you shouldn't do that.* Instead, Zara seemed to wait. I managed a nod, and she leaned closer. "You're so pretty, Emerald," she told me, and her lips brushed mine when she spoke, like a butterfly kiss. I'd always wanted a kiss like that, one that said, *We can take our time.* When my arms went around her, our chests touched, and Zara's nipples were tight little buttons.

"Lay down. Here." Zara pulled me to the moss. It smelled earthy, like good, rich soil. Somehow, that made everything better —like the forest had built us a little hideaway. Brush bowed above us; leaves rustled, whole stories sung by the wind. Zara's legs tangled into mine.

Her palm rested against my cheek, and she kissed me like I was something beautiful, breakable. My fingers wove into her long hair. Zara's lips were more delicate than any guy's, and kinder. I tried to think about that, not her long thigh pressed between mine. Mine pressed her too, and I couldn't think about that soft heat either. As her hand trailed down my neck to my back, I dared to pet her side, a perfect in-and-out curve. I'd wanted it forever. Her hip was a revelation, her waist a dream. I couldn't help wiggling closer.

"I like this," she whispered, and her hand darted between us. When she cupped my breast, I sighed and arched my back. My shorts tightened, and their seam pressed my clit. As I rocked my hips, that sweet pressure slid over me. I was already getting wet.

Zara didn't rush. She drew my nipple into a peak, then thumbed it softly. When I brushed hers, it had tightened to a hard nub. I wanted to feel it between my lips, but I didn't know how to get there. Those feminine curves baffled me, like a puzzle whose pieces I couldn't decode. She must've known. "Like that," she said, words half a kiss. "You can do it harder."

When I pinched her nipple, she sighed and pressed against my leg. That warmth had become almost hot, and her pussy slipped against me. If her curves confused me, that part seemed unimaginable.

I wanted her so much, but other thoughts barged in. Zara hadn't told me much about herself—where she lived, how old she was. What if she just liked coming out here and hooking up? Maybe it wasn't me she liked. Maybe she liked anybody rather than somebody. When you're lonely, you'll latch onto anything. I couldn't stop wondering about that, and I pulled back.

"What?" Zara's arched brows drew together, an adorable confusion. "What's wrong?"

"Where d'you live?" I asked.

Her nose wrinkled. "I told you. Not far from here."

I forced myself to sit up. I wanted to keep kissing her, but fear rolled in my belly. If this wasn't something I wanted, better to figure that out right away. I had to say it. She might think I didn't like her, and only that gave me enough guts to speak. "I don't know much about you," I admitted.

"Oh, *Emerald.*" Her laughter was like wind in the trees. "You're so worried about so many things that don't matter. I swear, I really like you. Is that so hard to believe?"

"What if it was?" I asked. "If you liked me, you'd tell me more about you."

"Okay." She shoved up. Her dress bunched on her thighs, and those vines did go all the way up, at least as far as I could tell. "I'm boring. I feed the birds. Did you know there are ivory-billed woodpeckers way, way deep in the forest? People don't believe it but it's true. They're back there. They aren't gone."

I didn't know much about those, but I heard they were extinct. "Really?"

"Yeah. That's why we have to protect places like this. People think they can take and take and take. They think they can burn oil and kill trees and it won't matter. There are otters in these creeks. They won't live in polluted water. If we don't stop..." And she was off. Zara told me about people throwing trash from their cars, and dumping tires in the woods, and carving their names on trees. "There were so many fireflies once," she said. "You wouldn't believe it, Emerald. They'd all light up at once, and whole fields would turn bright as day."

Mama said once that when she was a little girl, she scooped fireflies into jars, and they lit her room all night long. Lower Congaree is famous for its fireflies—we're one of the only places on earth where they blink at the same time, and tourists come from far away to see them. Strange how one person's everyday is someone else's miracle. Zara was almost in tears describing those pretty bugs. When she mentioned Carolina parakeets, how we'd torn up forests and starved those flocks of rainbow birds, her tears spilled over.

I picked up her hand. "It's awful," I said.

"It's horrible." She swiped at her nose. "And no one cares, Emerald. They don't care about it at all. I'm so angry. No one listens."

The cicadas had gone quiet. No birds sang, and no squirrels scuffled in the leaves. Only the stream burbled, on and on and on. The world seemed to hush, like that moment between a lightning flash and thunder. *Everything's listening*, I thought, then brushed it away.

"I'll listen," I told Zara. I would've given her anything when her big green eyes went wet, tears like dew on her lashes. I tried not to think of those parakeets. I'd never heard of them, and it seemed like one more symptom of a terminal sickness.

"We lost the parakeets a long time ago," she said, as if I'd spoken aloud. "A long, long time ago. I can still be mad. It won't bring them back, but I don't care." She gave me a sad little smile. "Now you know what I care about, I guess."

"It's beautiful even if it hurts," I said before I thought.

"What d'you mean?" she asked.

I winced. I'd sound even stupider than I already had. Sometimes I was good at that. I'd given up trying to talk a long time ago. I'd say something important, and no one listened, or they laughed, or they said, *Oh Emmy, that doesn't matter*. You learn silence that way. You shut up and take what the world hands out. It's a lonely kind of life, but at least no one's laughing at you. "I mean seeing how much you care," I tried to explain. "It's beautiful, but it's sad that you're sad, I guess. I don't know. It was dumb."

"No." She touched my cheek again. "You're exactly right. Tell me what you love that much."

I wished for a hoodie, at least something I could draw my fists into. I planted my hand on the moss instead and tried to concentrate on its pillowy softness. "I don't know."

"There must be something. No one cares about nothing."

I didn't want to say it. She wouldn't understand. "It's selfish and weird."

"I bet it's not." Zara slid her hand to my wrist again. "Tell me. I promise not to judge whatever it is."

I took a deep breath, like a running leap into deep water—the kind where you jump and hope you won't hit bottom. "I care about being myself."

"What do you mean?" Zara asked, and I could've watched those green eyes forever. They were the kind of eyes that would look, and keep looking, and see the very worst things without closing.

"I care about making myself into someone I wanna be, not who people say I am." Maybe that was the best way to phrase it. I was more than Emmy, or Luna, or that girl who danced for money. I wasn't a welfare mooch or a whore. I was Emerald. "I wanna save enough money to leave my mama's house," I said, real fast, like I had to get it out fast or I'd lose my nerve. "I wanna be around people who know me, I guess? I wanna be someone I can be proud of." I turned around and lifted my shirt. "That's why I got this." I gestured at my tattoo. "It's all South Carolina but it's more than that, too. The palmetto's the state tree 'cause of that Revolutionary War battle. We had to learn about it over and over in school—you probably did too. The one with the fort made out of palmettos. When the British shot cannonballs at it, they bounced off. I wanna be like that, you know? The type of person that no one can hurt. And I like the moon 'cause it changes, but it's always the same. It's feminine, I guess. I don't know."

It was too much and I drew my knees to my chin. I'd never told anyone why I picked my tattoo. It seemed like too much to say, like

I'd pulled a secret from my chest and held it in my hands, a broken bird.

"That's a good tattoo." Zara trailed her fingers over it, like she was tracing it with her eyes shut. "Those are good things to want, Emerald. See? You do care about something. It's the most important thing to care about, too—yourself. If you could get another tat, what would you get?"

"No contest," I said right away. I'd already thought about it, but no way could I afford something so intricate—my palmetto had cost me more than I wanted to think about. "I'd get vines on my legs like yours."

"Would you?" She almost squealed. Far away, crows cawed. Leaves whispered riddles, and sunshine slid through the canopy. The whole world seemed happy.

"Yeah," I said. "I love the way the vines look, but it's more than that, too." I thought about how to say it. "I feel like I can be myself here. So I'd want those vines to remind me who I am. Which is kinda weird, 'cause you had them first, but I don't think it matters." I curled up a little more. "I could never afford them."

"You never know," Zara stood up. "Meet you tomorrow?"

My heart skidded, like it slipped inside my chest, and the world seemed sad again. "What? Already? But we were having fun."

"Gotta go, sorry, Emerald," Zara said, and one more time, I loved her saying my name.

"If you gimme your number, we can text," I said, then remembered that I'd stormed out without my phone. "If you have yours, I'll put mine in, and—"

"Don't have anything with me," she said. "And I'll never remember your number. I'm terrible at numbers. You can meet me again, right?" She caught her lip between her teeth. I wanted to kiss it again. "See you tomorrow, Emerald."

"Where d'you *live*?" I called, but she was already bouncing down the trail. "Do you have a name on Insta or something, where I can message? Zara?"

She was already gone. The swamp had come alive again, crows cawing, cicadas whirring, a woodpecker tap-tapping far away. It reminded me of the ivory-bill. As I walked back to the house, I thought about the ivory-bill, and I thought about those parakeets. Mostly, I thought about that anger in Zara's eyes, her set jaw and tight lips. She cared about something, and that was worth everything.

MAMA AND AUNT Tabby came home and left again. On Friday nights, they hit The Roadhouse for margarita pitchers. Mama always said it was their one good time, and she'd met all our daddies there—not that she didn't know them already. Better to say she hooked up with our daddies there, but I hated thinking about my mama that way. I always wished my parents were married, or at least that Mama had married someone, sometime. When your parents are married, you don't have to think, *Did he really like her? Did he just bang her and walk away, and if he did, did she really want me?* Diamond and Jett and I never talked about it, probably 'cause Mama didn't. You don't want to think that you owe your whole existence to someone kinda drunk and horny, or about the cussing your mama did when her period didn't come. We'd never tell Diamond's baby that she wouldn't be there but for a clinic without any appointments. They said Diamond could drive to Virginia. We'd never tell her little girl, *If Aunt Emmy hadn't dropped her savings on a tattoo two months before your mama got knocked up—which your gramma loves to remind her about—then*

you wouldn't exist. That baby would figure it out one day. Kids always did.

With Mama and Aunt Tabby gone, my sister didn't have a chance to snitch. I barely saw her, anyway; she was passed out cold when I came in. Sweaty and tired, I took my own nap, dressed, and left for work. Alyssa was on, so it was better than most nights—someone to watch my back. We worked groups of guys together and raked in more money that way.

"How you been, Emmy?" she asked after last call, while we changed out of our dance clothes. "I've seen you all night, and we never had a chance to talk."

"Okay," I told her, 'cause she couldn't know about Zara. "Diamond's a bitch but what else is new?"

Alyssa laughed. She was what my gramma called a generous laugher, and I loved that about her. "Diamond's been bitching since she could talk. I swear her first words were 'I'm telling.' How's she feeling?"

"Same," I said. When Alyssa got knocked up, she went baby-crazy. Everything was "Lucky got a tooth," or "Lucky learned to crawl," or "I gotta take Lucky to his WIC appointment." He was almost a year old, and he'd stolen my best friend. It's weird to say that about a baby, but it's true. Before Alyssa got knocked up, we'd hang out all the time. She'd still smoke up, but only when the baby was asleep, and we had to be real quiet or we'd wake him. Lucky was cute, like every other baby, but he drooled and cried like every other baby, too. Hopefully I'd be out by the time Diamond's came. But my car would die, and I'd be socking away money to fix it, so I'd best plan on some earplugs.

"She pick any names yet?" Alyssa asked.

"She likes Mercedes and Porsche." I screwed my face into a yuck. "I said people already called her white trash, and she told me to shut my mouth."

Alyssa laughed again. "You got any plans for tomorrow?"

"Nah," I said. *I'm gonna see this girl I really like*, I wanted to tell her. Alyssa might not care that bi girls exist, but if I told her I was one of them, she'd think, *Was Emmy looking at me? Does she want to mess around?* She'd hate me after that. Maybe I was wrong, but Alyssa was the best friend I had. I couldn't risk it. We'd known each other since the first day of kindergarten—you don't throw that away, not if you can help it. "You maybe wanna do something Sunday night?" I asked.

"Can't hang out, I'm working," she told me, yanking a shirt over her head. "Lucky needs new shoes."

I should've known it had to do with the baby. Everything had to do with the baby anymore. *You know she'll be busy, Emmy*, Aunt Tabby had told me. *You gotta get used to not seeing her.*

That'll never happen, I said. *She'll always make time. We been friends since we were five.*

Aunt Tabby started to say something else, and Mama laid a hand on her shoulder. *She'll find out*, Mama told her, and that was all. I hated that they turned out right.

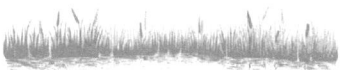

IN THE MORNING, I woke up again to Diamond's snoring. Our air conditioner hid the morning sun, so the room was gray and sad, all clumped dirty clothes and tattered posters from my high school years. I left them up 'cause I didn't want the walls bare. That would've been its own kind of loneliness, and I had enough of that in my life. I stumbled into the bathroom and turned on the shower. When I leaned down to take off my shorts, I almost fell.

Black vines climbed my ankles. They twined my calves, tangled behind my knees, and wrapped my thighs before disappearing under my shorts. I yanked my clothes off. Those vines reached my lower belly, and they were identical to Zara's.

They looked like tattoos.

I flashed back to the night before—work, no drinking, no drugs, not unless someone spiked my drink, and if that had happened, I wouldn't remember driving home and dropping into bed. I reached for that memory and found it clear as glass: Diamond snorfling, tripping on a dirty shirt, thinking about Zara and wishing my sister wasn't across the room so I could get myself off. I didn't visit a tattoo parlor, and tats as involved as those vines would've taken hours and hours, not counting a drive to Columbia.

I licked my finger and rubbed my leg. Those vines didn't smear. Panic beat in my chest, a frightened sparrow, and I trembled on the edge of hyperventilating from fear and hyperventilating for fear of hyperventilating. Those marks weren't going away. Those marks were etched on my skin like—I wouldn't think that word. "Breathe," I whispered to myself, and even that simple little word helped, spoken aloud like a spell. I closed my eyes and pictured the safest place I could, that swamp spread around me, all green and growing things. It would smell like honeysuckle. Like Zara—my breath kicked into panting, and I had to start all over again. *You're safe,* I told myself. *You're ten years old, and your gramma is hugging you tight. She's showing you how to bake real cornbread. It tastes sweet and buttery, like a promise, and you believe it. You will always be safe and loved. Breathe.*

I clenched my thighs, squeezed my eyes shut, and remembered Gramma, her cushy chest and warm, sweet smell. She'd say she was fat, but I liked her that way. When I was little, I thought people were only fat if my hands didn't touch when I reached around them. That memory, more than anything else, brought me back. I'd been so sure of my rightness, and so proud, 'cause I came up with that rule myself.

I opened my eyes. The cold tile chilled the soles of my feet. I was alone.

I let my head lean against the wall and thought. Water rushed from the faucet. It seemed like a sure, normal thing, like the cool floor under my hand, or those silk sleepy shorts. Sun leaned through the blinds, high and white, past noon; the bathroom smelled like wet towels left to sit til they molded.

Tattoos didn't just appear. It'd be magic if they did, and magic wasn't real. I'd met a few gothy girls who swore it was, but they'd say, *I cast a money spell and won ten dollars on my scratch-off ticket*, or *I did a love spell and so-and-so slept with me*. They made magic from coincidences and wishful thinking. Miracles, real ones —they're for kids and Bible-bangers. You cling to them when you don't have anything else, and they give you hope in a world dead-set against you.

They said Talitha could do something like magic. When doctors couldn't fix something, and someone got healed anyway, maybe that was a kind of magic, but not this kind. Lower Congaree said Talitha could do lots more than that—summon snakes, talk to ghosts, maybe even kill people. But Lower Congaree lives to sit on porches and spin tales. You can't believe people around here. They think their Power Ball numbers are bound to come up eventually. These days, God's short on miracles, so they look to what they have.

One more time, I spit on my finger and scrubbed at my leg. That ink didn't move, so I rubbed harder. A permanent marker would've dulled. My chest tightened, like something vital crumpling up too small. I rubbed so hard I almost tore my skin, and I couldn't feel those lines at all. They were as smooth as tattoos healed a year before.

If you could get any tattoo, what would it be? Zara had asked.

No contest. I'd get vines like yours. But I could never afford them.

You never know, she'd said. I remembered her smile, how it had curved higher on one side. It'd seemed sweet then, but altogether different now—a little more sinister, like a stranger offering candy. Were those tats supposed to be a gift, a magic one, like something in a fairy tale? Fairy-tale presents came with heavy price tags. If you want the boy, you give the sea witch your voice. If you're born gorgeous, your stepmother tries to murder you. There's always a price, and no matter how good the deal sounds, it's always more than you're willing to pay. Anyway, there is no once-upon-a-time. And even if there was, no handsome prince or princess was coming to my rescue. I'd known that since I was eight.

I rubbed the red spot on my thigh, rubbed it hard enough to curl my skin into little balls. My thigh burned, and when the skin came up I knew those were tattoos. They weren't coming off. They were permanent; they were mine; and they'd happened after I met Zara in that swamp. That meant one of two things was true—either Zara put them there, or the swamp did.

You don't wanna go in that swamp, Talitha told me. *There's no one you wanna meet there, and people come back changed.*

I thought she meant mind-different, not body-different. I examined those vines then, really looked at them. Just like Zara's, they were a real artist's work, all delicate lines and shading. They twisted and curled, folded and crimped—*tendrilled*, that was the vocabulary word. They tendrilled up my legs. They twined my inner thighs, and I'd have remembered that part—thinking about needles there made me wince. I bent my leg up like the cheerleader I'd never been. The vines went all the way around, just as complicated on the back as the front. They were stunning. No artist in Columbia, South Carolina could've done that, not any I knew.

Maybe you oughta be grateful, I thought for a second, then shoved it back. I tried not to love them. But when I climbed on the toilet and looked at my legs in the medicine cabinet mirror, those vines were exactly how I'd have wanted them. That made about as much sense as the tats appearing in the first place. Real life never lives up to imagination.

I couldn't keep them secret. If I wore pants, everyone would ask why, and I had to take my clothes off at work. News would get around. Diamond would hear about them, and she'd tattle like a ten-year-old. I couldn't hide them, not if I wanted to keep my job.

No way in hell was I working in that chicken plant.

I met this girl in the swamp. Her tats appeared on my legs. Not only did it sound insane, if Mama *did* believe me, she'd say, *Well, I told you not to go back there. This is your fault. Maybe you learned your lesson, Emmy Ann.*

I stood up. Sometimes, that's all you can do. I might've been close to hyperventilating, all gasping breath and shaking hands, but life goes on, I guess. Seeing real magic knocked me flat, but you can't stay flat forever. You have to stand up, and you have to get in the shower, and you have to wash your legs and think: *These are mine. My legs didn't have tattoos but now they do. I don't know how that ink got there, but I can't scrub them off, so I have to live with them.*

I washed hard, too. My legs turned red. Soap and water were my last hope, and those vines stayed. I turned off the creaky faucet and snagged a towel from the floor. It had probably sat there for days, but I'd forgotten to grab one from my room. I tried not to smell it. Then I almost laughed. Magic tattoos appeared on my legs, and I worried about stinky towels. No, I corrected myself. Like Zara said, nothing disappears. So nothing just appears, either; those tats came from Zara or the swamp, one or the other. My panic settled into bone-deep fear. Once I wished that swamp would show me something magic. I'd hoped for a bobbing orb or a talking crow. Maybe I wanted those tats, but I didn't want them *that* way.

Mama was gonna lose her mind, and I couldn't do a damn

thing about it. I could only hold on and pray. So I threw on some shorts, braced myself, and walked into the storm.

Aunt Tabby was flipping pancakes. Mama hunched at the table with a cup of coffee—you don't want to think about your own mother hungover, but she might've been. "Morning," Jett said, looking up from his scrambled eggs. "Hey! That's some nice ink. When did you get that?"

Mama snapped up. "What ink?" I saw her noticing—her eyes got wide, her mouth dropped open, her coffee cup froze in mid-air. "Emerald Ann Joiner," she said, and that quiet anger was meaner than any yelling. "How fucking much did you spend on that?"

"My friend did it. It didn't cost anything." I dropped to a chair. Maybe the fight would pass quicker if she couldn't see my legs. "And before you ask, I met her at work." While I was changing, I'd ginned up a whole story about how that friend was Lexie Smith, and I'd met her at the club. She was training to be a tattoo artist. You have to know your backstory. If your details don't match, or someone asks a question and you take too long to answer, they'll catch you out for sure. Luckily—for once—the family thought I was too dumb to think up much of anything. *She's not the brightest bulb, but Lord knows she does her best*, Mama would say. I couldn't shoot back, *Well, I'd've done better, but me and Alyssa skipped class to smoke pot in the bathroom.*

"Your friend did it. You gonna tell me you got a kitchen tattoo?" Mama slammed her coffee down so hard that some spilled out. "How many times have I told you—"

"She sterilized everything!" I protested, like it was God's honest truth.

"You think you looked like trash before?" Mama dropped back to that soft, dangerous voice. "You look like you walked outta a cathouse. When I was coming up, the only people with tattoos were whores and sailors, and I don't see a fucking boat."

"Mama—" I started, and my voice had an edge that startled me.

"Don't you even try it," she snapped. "I know what people are gonna think of you. They'll say I raised you wrong. You know that, don't you?" The ugliness started. I knew what she'd say: *You look like a tramp. You look like a slut.* She'd call me every bad thing you could say about a girl, all while Aunt Tabby nodded. Sometimes she'd add, *That's right,* or *Uh-huh,* like Mama was preaching a Sunday sermon.

I wouldn't listen to it again. Instead of shame, anger bloomed in my chest, green and strong and bright. "I know what you're gonna say," I told her. "You can save it. I got these tats and I like 'em. You wanna kick me out like Aunt Tabby kicked out Jackson? Go ahead. I dance. I don't fuck for money, no matter what you say, and at least I don't come home smelling like chicken shit."

Mama stared. There were some things you didn't do, and one of them was talk back.

"Y'all are mad 'cause I want something more than what you got," I said. "Too damn bad."

"Emerald Ann Joiner." Mama breathed my name like a cuss word. "Don't you take that tone with me, girl."

"I'll talk however I want," I told her, and it felt good, righteous and holy. "I'll—"

Diamond wandered in. Mama's shouting probably woke her up. "You know Emmy was in that swamp yesterday, too," she said. "I saw her go back there."

"You did not. When d'you think I got those tattoos done? They took hours and hours. I didn't have time to mess around in the swamp, even if I wanted to."

"Your car was still here." Diamond crossed her arms over that big belly, like impending motherhood lent her an authority I'd never have.

"That's 'cause my friend picked me up!" I had that part ready, too. I knew Diamond would pile on—some people are just that predictable.

"You were out in that swamp again?" Mama's voice rose to a shout. "Goddammit, I told you not to go out there! Didn't Talitha tell you the same thing?"

That question had no right answer—a yes would have her asking why I didn't listen, and no would get me called me a liar. I kept quiet.

"Well?" Mama planted her hands on her hips like I was five years old.

My brave anger withered and died. I could've described the whole scene before it happened—Mama shouting, Aunt Tabby nodding, my brother and sister hoping Mama didn't drag them into it. She'd say Jett was lazy, and Diamond an irresponsible hoochie mama. It would be funny if Mama wasn't serious. She'd say she loved us, but sometimes I wondered. What does love mean? When I was little, I thought it meant feeding someone and giving them clothes. As I got older, I thought maybe there was more to it. Maybe love was listening and holding someone when they were sad. That food-and-clothes thing was part of it, but love meant a whole lot more. It took me a long time to learn that. If that was true—and I knew it was—did anyone love me? Gramma had, but she was gone. No one knew I was bi, and maybe that was my answer. My eyes stung. When I started to cry, Mama said, "You go on and cry your eyes out, Emmy Ann, 'cause you know I'm telling the truth."

Sunshine struggled through the narrow kitchen window, but it promised a glorious summer day. It seemed unfair that Mama ruined such a pretty morning. I wished it was raining, or at least cloudy, but the sun went on shining. It always does. The world never stops for our disasters. That seemed like the most unfair thing of all.

EVENTUALLY, I fled to my room. Even Diamond left me alone. I heard them watching something in the living room, a dumb show about rich people being rich. I never understood why everyone gawks at millionaires. Those shows leave you envious and sad, remembering that you're poor and always will be. You wish for more than you've got, and it'll hurt you if you think too hard. Those people, they're only famous 'cause they're rich or weird. No one would make a show about us Joiners. Or maybe they would. The world could learn how to feed five people on food stamps.

I curled on my bed and played games on my phone. If I went into the living room, they'd harass me. If I left the house, they'd say, *Where're you going, Emmy Ann? Don't you get another one of those fucking kitchen tattoos.* I wanted to visit Zara. I never wanted to see her again. Either she'd given me those tats or the swamp had, and either way, I wasn't walking back there again.

I tried to concentrate on Wordscapes. It didn't work. I was staring down real magic. In fairy tales, people accept it as part of the scenery. They never freak out, like magic is something different and wild, like if you look too hard, you'll see the world broke open and bloody at your feet. It could've made me insane if I thought too hard.

I yanked my shorts off and looked at my vines, really looked at them, then stood on my bed and examined them in Diamond's dresser mirror. They twined my legs just like Zara's, straight in my underwear, like a promise of something I might not want to give. Drawing the eye right between my legs, it felt like someone could grab hold of them and climb on up. I twisted around and near about hurt my neck trying to see how they looked from behind. For a snatched moment, I thought they were getting thicker. *They aren't*, I assured myself. *You're not used to seeing them.*

I wasn't. Would I ever be? Under my fingers, they were as smooth as tats done months before. I couldn't decide if they'd earn me more money or less. Some guys hated tats. Mostly, though, gothy ones could get away with it. But whatever they were, however they'd appeared, those vines were stunning, art someone would pay thousands and thousands for. *I'd get vines like yours. But I could never afford them.*

I fucking loved them. Dropping to my bed, I curled up. It was too much to think about, too scary. So what if I loved them? They were magic. Gifts were never free. If people gave you something, you owed them something in return. That's how the world worked. It always had. "Lookit all those presents, Emmy Ann," Mama always said on Christmas, when one church or another dropped off gifts. "You better do well in school and make me think you deserve them."

"Yes, ma'am," I'd reply. As tears rose, the Christmas lights would go blurry. Those presents weren't presents at all. They were promises, agreements: *You give me this, and I'll give you that.*

You can waste a whole day on your phone. You don't even have to try.

When I finally got ready for work, Mama and Aunt Tabby were gone. On the saggy, secondhand couch, Diamond and Jett were watching one of those shows about naked people stranded on an island. "Where're you going?" my sister asked. Her eyes didn't move from the TV, all naked butts, and her hand didn't leave that bag of chips. Apparently, if they put you on prime time, it's okay to take off your clothes.

"You know damn well where I'm going," I said.

Diamond snorted. She'd only spoken up so she could start a fight. "You're gonna go shake your ass for money, that's what you're gonna do."

Jett sank lower. He hated when we fought, and he hated when they talked about my job. I ignored Diamond and grabbed a banana from the kitchen table.

She couldn't let me go that easy. "How d'you think Jett feels when the guys at school say they saw you naked?"

"They don't—" Jett started, then shut up. He never could stand up to her.

I peeled my banana and took a bite, but I couldn't taste it. I was tired of taking shit from her. I refused to pluck dead chickens til my hands ached. *You're doing great, Emmy*, they should've said. *You don't have much, but you use what you got.* I was gonna get myself outta that house, maybe even that town. I didn't know where I'd go, but it'd be bigger, brighter, full of people who never did or said a boring thing. There would be lesbians, and trans people, and bi people and gay people and everyone in between. They'd hold hands on the street, and people would smile. I'd be more than they ever thought I could be, more than that airless box they squished me into. Light cracked through my broken places then. Call it strength, maybe, a power twining around my ribs and tangling my chest. Suddenly, I wanted to smash life open. I wanted to leave it red and weeping at my feet.

"Least I'm not pregnant," I told Diamond. "Dancing lasts one night, and pays money besides. You'll be stuck with that baby for eighteen years. You still wanna make me ashamed? See how it feels in four months when you're digging through the couch cushions for diaper money."

Her hand went over her belly. "It's not gonna be like that," my sister said, and a little bit of that mean turned scared. "It's not."

"Uh-huh." They could see my new tattoos and I didn't care. "Why's it not gonna be like that? 'Cause you're getting diapers from the food bank? Jett's smart enough to wrap it up, and he's only fifteen. You were too stupid to do it when you were twenty-three. Now you're making the rest of us pay for it. Call me a whore if you want, but you're the one who got in trouble for fucking." I spoke in the same cold, angry voice Mama used on me.

"Shut up," Diamond said, her eyes filling. "Stop it, Emmy Ann."

"No, if I stop it you'll call me a whore again," I snapped back. The TV babbled on, people trying to make do when they had nothing left. "Good for you for keeping that baby, if that's what you wanted. I mean it, too. But don't call me names for making my own choices."

"You go to hell." She swiped at her face. "You know I didn't want a baby."

"Well, your choices got you one," I said. "And I'm sorry for that. But don't take it out on me. Don't take it out on Jett, either, 'cause as soon as I walk outta here, that's what you're gonna try."

Thank you, Jett mouthed.

"You're welcome," I told him. Grabbing my purse, I picked up my keys and left.

All that anger had finally come out, like I knew it would one day. I always worried I'd choke on it. *You did good, Emerald*, I imagined Zara saying. *You did exactly right.* Then I remembered I'd never tell her about it, and all that strength drained away. Sadness hunched in its place. Zara knew I liked girls. When I was with her, I didn't have to pretend.

It didn't matter. Those tattoos had appeared overnight, and I'd best stay away from her, stay away from that swamp. Magic scared me, and even if it didn't, I'd owe a price I could never pay. Zara might try to collect it, and I didn't want to think about what that might mean.

If I cried, I'd ruin my makeup, so I counted breaths instead. When I turned onto the highway, the swamp closed in, all green, braided vines. Even through the rushing wind, I heard its cicadas humming. Damn Zara. I wasn't in love with her, I told myself. You can't be in love with a person you saw twice in your life. But if I had to name that feeling, the word *love* came closest.

I pulled into the club's dust-dry parking lot. *Breathe*, I ordered myself. *Take two deep breaths and forget about it.* I'd done that when my daddy left. Five years old, I'd been hiding around the living room corner when he slammed out our front door. Mama thumped onto the couch and fell into strangling sobs that could've torn me open like a rag doll. *You can't cry*, I'd thought then. *Be sad for two deep breaths, then forget about it.* Maybe I'd heard that on one of Mama's shows, those endless soap operas with people always dying and fighting and poisoning each other. So I took two shuddery breaths and set it aside. I'd been startled at how well it worked. Kids figure out how to survive, I guess. Their insides fray, and they learn to hide the tattered places.

I drew two deep breaths, then walked across that hot, gritty parking lot. As usual, guys hung around the club's black door. One was poking through the ashtray and pretending not to. He couldn't afford cigarettes, so he was smoking someone else's butts.

"Hey, honey," said a skeletal guy with too much acne. "What're you up to tonight?"

"Dancing," I replied as I passed.

He leaned on the dirty wall. "Maybe you wanna go home with me instead."

"Maybe I don't fuck methheads," I shot back. Usually I'd only think something like that, and it startled me as much as him.

His friend laughed. I pushed the door open and stepped from day to that strange, timeless night. Mirrors reflected the Christmas lights, someone's sad ideas of stars. No one was dancing. Bass thumped like a second heartbeat, and a few men scattered the chained-down tables. No girls were on yet, but they would be soon.

I caught Noah's face as he saw my tats. His nose wrinkled, and his forehead furrowed, and he ducked down fast, maybe hoping I wouldn't see. He hated them. Instead of sagging, though, I squared my shoulders. They weren't his, and they weren't *for* him. They weren't for anyone. I hadn't done them, but I'd asked for them, and they were mine. I loved them.

"What d'you think of the tats?" I asked, sliding onto a barstool.

He smiled, but it didn't reach his eyes. You can always tell a fake smile. I'd seen too many of them. "I like them if you like them," he told me.

"Thanks," I said, and he slid me a Coke. "A friend of mine did 'em."

"Be careful." He held up a finger to a customer: *I'll be there in a sec.* "If you just got them done, they'll be tender today. Don't mess with that."

I was that girl who followed all the aftercare instructions. I washed new tats three times a day, patted them dry, and rubbed them with Desitin. If those vines were new, I'd have been wrapped in plastic-y bandages, laid up in the air conditioning, and sure as hell not about to dance. "I'll be careful," I told Noah.

"You don't wanna scar 'em." Noah fussed below the bar, like I might see too much in his face if he stood up. "Who did those? I've been looking for a good artist."

"My friend Lexie's an apprentice." I scrunched up my nose. "She lives down in Miami. Left just before I came in today." I had to pick somewhere far away, too far for him to travel.

"Too bad." He gave me one of those grins that don't quite sit straight. "Well, lemme know if you need some aspirin for them, okay? Helps take down inflammation."

"I will," I said. Hefting my bag, I threaded backstage. I could feel all those men watching me. They were wondering what I'd look like naked. *Let them look*, I thought. *Let them see what they're gonna pay for.* I strode slower, from my hips, and if they weren't staring at my ass before, they watched then. In heels, covered in long, winding vines, my legs looked a million miles long. I imagined them with those jean shorts that barely covered my ass, and I wished Zara could see. Our legs would've looked so pretty tangled together. I'd missed seeing her. She would've waited at our spot all afternoon. *Two deep breaths*, I told myself as I pictured her worrying, then getting up and walking home alone. *Two deep breaths, Emmy.* Even if I wanted to forget her, those tattoos would never let me.

Alyssa squealed when I stepped into the dressing room—trust her to notice right away. "Oh my God, when did you get *those* done?" she asked. "Emmy, those are gorgeous!"

"Thanks," I said, and we went through the who-did-those, she's-from-Miami talk. I told Alyssa the artist was a friend of Jackson's friend. 'Cause of the pot dealing, she stayed away from him; they'd take Lucky if she got caught near a dealer.

At the bottom of my bag, I found those booty shorts I never dared to wear, black with shiny-buckled garters. When I pulled them out, Alyssa asked, "Are you gonna wear *them?* Emmy, that'll look awesome."

"Yeah," I said, and after I tied on a black bikini top, I added a body harness I'd never tried, either. The collar strapped around my neck, and a chain led to the buckle below my boobs. I'd always wanted to try it, but I never quite had the courage.

"It looks killer, but are you sure it'll be okay rubbing those new tats?" Alyssa turned around, and I tied her string bikini.

"They'll be fine. I lotioned them up real well, and the girl who did them said they'd be okay." I glanced in the mirror. Vines arched just above my shorts and dipped down again. I'd never wear garters again, at least not any that started at my ankles. My legs were stunning on their own.

Alyssa went out first. When she finished, the DJ started Nine Inch Nails's "Starfuckers, Inc.," and I strode onstage. Instead of staring into the dark, I focused on the men next to the stage. Then I planted my back against the pole and grabbed above my head. As the lyrics kicked in, I squatted down, hands sliding with me, then back up, and I was gone. For once I didn't think about what those men were thinking, or if I danced well, or how much I wished for an audience of girls. *Let them want what they can't have*, I thought. *Let them wish for it, and let them pay for those wishes*. Spinning and twisting, I lost myself in that dance. Guys tucked money in my harness, in my garters. When I crouched on the edge of the stage, they whispered in my ear, and I laughed.

"Let's grab a room," said an older guy. I might've recognized him, maybe someone's dad. It should've icked me out.

"Sure, honey," I said.

I spent most of the night drinking wine with him—the first time I drank at work—in one of those curtained boxes that count as private rooms. Of course, he asked if I'd do more than dance. "That's illegal," I laughed, and he didn't bring it up again. Those rooms cost a hundred an hour—twenty-five to the house, seventy-five to me. I walked outta there with three hundred dollars and two hours left before closing. I hadn't thought of Zara the whole time. I might've been more grateful for that than the money.

"Good job," Noah said afterward, pushing a Coke in my direction.

"Thanks," I told him.

"Great dance, earlier. If I'd've been in the front row, you'd've taken all my money." He gave me a crooked grin. I smiled back. If he wasn't my boss, I might've flirted back.

"I think I cleaned a few of them out," I replied, absolutely serious. When I checked my thong after that dance, I found a twenty.

"You sure you don't want any rum in that?" He gestured at my drink.

"Nah," I said. "I'm about to hit the floor."

"Your car running okay?" Alana's "Get Low" kicked on, and

Noah leaned his elbows on the bar. "It was making a funny noise when you pulled out the other night. I can always pick you up, y'know? Don't drive something that might get you hurt." Noah's brown hair looked messier than usual, and under the Christmas lights, his eyes were wide and dark. He was cute, if you were into that.

"Thanks," I said, draining the rest of my drink. "Imma get dancing. Lemme know if you need anything." I left the empty Coke on the bar. My Nissan had bald tires and a wonky air conditioner; God only knew what was wrong under the hood. I expected it to die every time I stuck the key in. Noah was so sweet. Hopefully I wouldn't need his offer, but if I did, it'd keep me outta that chicken plant.

Back on the floor, I plopped down next to some lonely guys and scored some dances. About an hour later, I kissed one on the cheek and hopped to the floor. After hustling my ass off, I was ready for a bathroom trip and a breather. The day had sunken too late or too early, depending on your point of view, and the club was dropping into that sad hour of solo guys and hard drinkers, men who'd whisper and sag over their liquor. They'd want to talk about their emptiness instead of buying dances. Sometimes, they'd cry. When that happened, I'd pat their backs and tell them it wasn't that bad, not really. I was always lying.

"Hey." A hand closed over my wrist. The Wheeler kid's breath smelled worse than before. "Where you going, girl?"

I shook him off. "What, you gonna wait at the door like a creeper and try to ambush me again?" I spoke loud over the music, loud so guys nearby could hear. "Don't touch me, you sick-ass motherfucker."

A guy at a nearby table stood. His chair screeched over the sticky floor like a challenge, and he had to be six-three, all beefed-out football muscle. "Is this guy bothering you, ma'am?"

"He sure as hell was bothering her the other night." Noah

loomed over the Wheeler kid, who shrank into his seat. He was the type of guy who bullied women when he could get away with it, but backed down like a kicked dog when he couldn't. I knew that type. They made up two-thirds of the men in Lower Congaree.

"He's not bothering me anymore," I told Noah. "Thanks. He was just leaving, I think." Then I smiled at the big guy. "I'll be right back, sweetie. Save me a spot on your lap."

"You heard her," Noah said as I walked away. "Get the fuck out or I'll make you wish you had. And don't you wait around in that parking lot, Isaac. I'll put your head through this table if something happens to her, and I'll tell your preacher daddy why I did it, too."

It was that easy. I'd never known, or maybe I'd been too scared to try it. That power bloomed between my ribs again, the feeling I had when I told off Diamond. That night, I left with four hundred and fifty dollars, double what I usually pulled in, and I kissed Noah's cheek as he walked me out.

"Thanks again," I told him.

"Be safe, Emmy," he replied, a hand resting on my shoulder. "Lemme know if anyone bothers you."

He'd never called me Emmy before. My car started, and I waved as I drove out. I might not have had Zara, but someone was watching my back. That lost, sad ache settled again. I wished I could tell Zara about that night. *I was brave*, I'd have said. *They loved my tats, and I wasn't scared.*

You should always be that brave, she'd say. *It wasn't the tattoos. It was you, Emerald.*

She'd touch my cheek, and I'd believe it.

I was off Sunday. Everyone else went to church, even Jett—Mama and Aunt Tabby liked the Holiness church. I stopped going the first time Mama spoke in tongues. Shouting nonsense, she fell down on the floor, and even though it looked like another flavor of normal there, I wanted to die from the shame of it. It sort of broke my heart at the same time, too. Mama speaking in tongues was a kind of wishful thinking, not that she necessarily faked it. Those people wanted God to touch them so badly that they thought he actually had. I didn't believe Jesus and his angels watched us from heaven. If he did, I hated him. Think of all that power. He wouldn't even drop in to fix Mama's back, bent up and hurting from a dozen years of plucking chickens. He let people die, and hurt little kids, and do all the terrible things that people do so often they blend into the scenery. He could've fixed it. So like hell was I watching Mama fall down and claim he was behind it all.

If Jesus was real, he was sending me to hell. Why go to church? The old people whispered about me behind their hands, and I could read it on their faces: *Emmy Ann Joiner has sex for money*. Better to stay home alone, wishing for something to believe in.

After breakfast, I wandered to the front porch for a smoke. Everything seemed motionless, stuck in heat-soaked stillness. I felt like I was waiting for the world to begin again. Lighting a cigarette, I slumped in a dry-rotted lawn chair. I could've been the last person on Earth.

I thought about that, what I'd do if I was totally alone, how I'd break into the stores and try on all the clothes, then make myself filet mignon for dinner. I'd never had it, but it sounded nice. I was still thinking about that when an old orange car drove around the corner. That movement felt like a miracle. It pulled into the drive, and Talitha rolled down the window farther. Wind had blown her dark hair messy. She didn't wear makeup, but she didn't need any.

"Hey, Emmy!" she called. "Tell your mama I stopped by, will you?"

"You can stay til she comes," I said, 'cause it was the polite thing to do. Mama would be home in about half an hour. I didn't want to spend my morning with Talitha Merle, but it didn't look like I had a choice. "You want a smoke?"

She turned off the car and climbed out. "Yeah," she replied. "I haven't had one in a long time." I handed her a cigarette, and she took the other rickety chair. "Damn, but this is good," she said. "Nothing like smoking outside on a hot summer morning."

She was right, though I'd never put it into words. There was something good about that stillness, watching those trees hang motionless and smoking my first cigarette of the day.

"Nice tats," Talitha told me. "When did you get those?"

"The other day," I replied. It wasn't a lie.

She squinted. "They look real healed up."

"Guess so." There wasn't much else I could say. Those tats looked real healed up 'cause no one had stuck needles in me. Maybe I was lucky, maybe cursed. I'd managed not to think about it that morning.

"Huh." Talitha didn't say anything else, like she'd decided to let me keep my secrets.

We were alone. If I didn't have enough courage to ask then, I never would. The only bi girl I'd ever met was Zara. I wondered if there was an underground place to go, or a code so secret it wasn't on the internet. I'd looked. *How do you know*, I wanted to ask. *And once you know, how do you ask if she likes you?* "I don't wanna bring up anything bad," I said carefully. "But Mama and Aunt Tabby were talking one time, and they said that even though you're married now, you went out with girls before."

Talitha glanced at me quick, surprised, then smiled. "Never tried to keep it a secret. You too, huh?"

My eyes must've gone deer-in-the-headlights. She laughed.

"Don't worry," she told me. "I only knew 'cause you mentioned it. I'm right, aren't I?"

"Don't tell, please?" I asked. She'd scared me for a moment, like I had it written on me and everyone could see. "Mama would lose her mind. It's one thing if it's you and another if it's her own daughter."

"Lord, I know what that's like." Talitha looked at the trees across the road, a dark, unknowable tangle. "I didn't go out with a girl til my mama passed." She seemed to think for a while, like she was remembering a girl, or maybe remembering that sick, trapped feeling, like being held underwater. "You ever gone out with a girl?" she asked eventually.

Talitha would know if I was lying. "Maybe," I said. "I don't know. I kissed her."

"Did you like her?" she asked.

I watched those tall, still trees. The swamp stretched beyond them—the whole town twined through swampland. When it rained too hard, roads flooded, and little creeks churned into angry rivers. We lived in it and with it. Maybe it fucked with us some, having that strange place so close. I wondered if life was different away from it. Maybe there were small differences I'd never notice unless I left. "The girl I kissed?" I said finally. "Yeah. I liked her a whole lot. They wouldn't believe me, though. They'd say I was fooling around and it wasn't serious, 'cause she's a girl."

"Did you want it to be serious?" Talitha asked.

"I think so," I replied. "Yeah. I think I did." I wanted it more than anything. I wanted to wake up next to Zara, all soft edges and curves. Morning sun would warm my face while I nuzzled into her neck. The tiny hairs there would tickle my nose, and she'd smell like home.

"What was the girl like?" Maybe Talitha was studying me. I didn't look.

"Pretty," I said right away. Now that we were talking, something about Talitha inspired trust, like I could hand her all my secrets. "But she was sweet, too. She listened. And she made me feel like I could be more than I was, y'know? More than other people see. They all think I have sex for money." I spit it like a curse. Suddenly my cigarette tasted ashy and bitter-sick. I mashed it under my flip-flop.

"I know they give you a hard time for dancing," Talitha said. "Did she?"

I was grateful she'd said dancing, not stripping. "No," I replied. "She knew, and she didn't care."

Talitha drew a long puff on her cigarette, then breathed out a rolling cloud of smoke. "So that girl was kind and she liked you for who you are. I should smack you silly. Why the hell did you let her go?"

"It's a long story," I said. "I sorta had to."

"No good reason for letting go of someone who sees you and loves you anyway." Talitha spoke as seriously as Mama's preacher, like I'd skipped church and found it waiting on the front porch.

I sagged, and my chair creaked under me. It'd fall apart soon. My car, the house—they'd fall apart, too. Sometimes it felt like the whole world was tumbling down, and I couldn't do a damn thing to stop it. "I had a good reason for letting her go."

The swamp seemed wrapped in quiet, like it was waiting for us to speak. I drank some water and lit another cigarette.

Talitha snagged another from my pack. "I went out with Charlotte Price for a few months," she said. "Long time back. She's married to Estlin Lanier now—y'know, the big-shot lawyer. Three kids." A little smile crept up her cheeks again. "She probably forgot all about me by now. Trust me, I remember her. But part of me was always shut off when we were together. She didn't want to hear about my life. She'd say it scared her. 'Don't talk about the people who need your help,' she'd tell me. If I was mixing up herbs for someone, she'd walk out. 'I don't wanna know what it's for,' she said once.

"So I eventually told her it wasn't working out. You can't be with someone who doesn't accept all of you. And when someone does, you hold on for dear life, Emmy. Those people are few and far between, and you don't let them go."

"I had to." My throat started to close, and my chest hurt. I wanted to tell her everything, but I didn't dare. *I told you so*, she'd say. *You don't mess with some things. You got yourself into this, and you can get yourself out.* That's what Mama would've said if she believed me. She wouldn't. I wouldn't have believed me either, so I couldn't hold it against her.

We quieted again. There was no wind, no birds, no squirrels dashing through their everyday business. I drew on my cigarette and concentrated on that ashy burn. It filled my lungs, and when I breathed it out, the smoke rolled up and away, one movement in all that motionless, stretched time.

"Huh," Talitha said again. "Does that girl have anything to do with your new tats? I'm sure as the day is long you didn't sit for 'em. They're too healed up—anyway, I saw your legs on Thursday, and I'd've noticed those tattoos."

I froze. Cigarette smoke hazed into the sky, and I thought about running. I thought about leaving Talitha there on that porch, slamming the door and hiding in my room. She'd have told Mama. I never should've offered her a cigarette.

But Talitha wasn't done. "You smell like magic, girl. It about slapped me in the face when I came up on this porch. You wanna tell me what's going on?"

"Nothing," I managed. "I don't know what you're talking about."

"Uh-huh." Talitha leaned back in her chair. I swear I felt her looking at me. "You gonna tell me you aren't up to some kinda magic?"

"No," I told her. Not a lie—I hadn't done the magic. Zara had. I dropped my cigarette and ground it out. I still had about half of it left, but my heart beat too hard, and I was almost dizzy.

"Emmy, you can tell me the truth." Talitha's voice turned kind —almost like she wanted to help. But no one ever helped, and she wasn't gonna lure me into that game. The sooner you learn that you're on your own, the better.

"Look, it's not every day that magic pops up in your life," she said after a long, settling silence. "If you want help, I'm here."

"Is it bad magic?" The question came before I could stop it. If she could tell me, I wanted to know.

Talitha nodded like she expected that question. "People talk about white magic and black magic all the time. Everyone's either Glinda the Good Witch or a straight-out Satanist. But there's no such thing as all-good or all-bad. Magic's the ultimate gray area, honey. Was it meant with kindness or malice? Does it make you do bad things?"

"No," I said. "I told someone I wanted these tats and could never afford them."

"There's your answer, then." Talitha's chair creaked as she got up. "Tell your mama I stopped by."

"I will," I said. "But—"

"No buts, Emmy." Talitha swished through the brown grass, sad and parched with summer, then climbed into her car. "You find that girl again, you hear me? She accepts you. You got anyone else who does that?"

"Other than you?" I asked, and she tipped me a wave as she pulled out. I went into the house. I didn't have anybody, not really. Life was lonely, but I figured everyone was lonely most of the time, so why not me? *Hold on for dear life, Emmy. Those people are few and far between, and you don't let them go.*

Maybe I had a chance at something. I turned on the shower. Those tattoos were beautiful. Maybe they were magic, but Zara had handed that magic to me. I didn't even believe in it, or at least I hadn't. It didn't matter. Zara knew who I was, and that was the best magic of all.

And so what if she could do things like that? Maybe people could, like Talitha, and I'd just never seen it. The whole world seemed bigger than I'd ever imagined then, huge and full of secrets. If Zara could paint tattoos on my legs, she could find me.

I showered, dressed, and walked into the swamp.

BIRDS WHISTLED IN THE TREES, and humidity hugged me close. The greens seemed brighter, and vines hung like birthday-banners. That swamp didn't seem like the same gray place surrounding our school playground, the woods kids pointed to and said, "You'll disappear if you go back there." Little birds flitted from branch to branch. Somewhere, a woodpecker drummed, and small creatures rummaged through the underbrush. Everything was alive and vivid, like I'd left a dull world behind and stepped into technicolor. I felt like Dorothy walking into Oz.

"You're here!" Zara bounced to her feet and threw her arms around me. I nuzzled into her neck and breathed her in. "Why didn't you come yesterday? I was so worried."

I tried not to think about that, about her waiting and watching the trail. At every sound, she'd have snapped up, looking and hoping. I've waited like that too many times. You sit and hope, and slowly, that hope turns to sadness. The knowledge comes bit by bit until you see it: Whatever you're waiting for, it's not coming, and that last little bit of hope dries up. You feel it crumbling, like a plant dying on a windowsill, leaves curling and brown. I hate that feeling more than almost any other.

"I was scared," I said. My lips brushed Zara's coppery neck. I'd cry if I imagined her waiting for me. "I woke up with tattoos, and it freaked me out, y'know?"

"You like them, right?" She drew back, and my arms went achingly empty. We sat down. "You said you wanted them. You said they'd make you feel more like you. I thought . . ." Blinking hard, she trailed off. "I'm sorry."

"I love them," I said quickly. "It was sweet of you. I just didn't expect it. Then I talked to someone, and she told me—well, she told me if I thought they were a gift, then they weren't bad. She said people who accept you are few and far between, and you need to hold on to them."

"I wanted you to have something beautiful." Zara's dark eyes were big, serious, maybe still close to tears. "Move your legs and let me see."

Obediently, I scootched over and stretched out, almost sighing at the cool moss pressing my legs. I could've stretched out and watched the leaves ruffle above us.

"Oooh." Zara traced my calf, and my breath caught. "Those look even better than mine."

She laid her head on my shoulder. It felt right, satisfying, like tossing a rock in the water and hearing its deep plop.

"The guys at work liked them," I said. "I bitched one out last night. When it happened I thought, 'Zara would be proud of me.'" Then I told her all the things I'd wanted to say—I told her about Mama, and my fight with Diamond, and Isaac Wheeler and how much money I'd made at work. "It almost felt like the tattoos helped," I said. "But how did you do them?"

Zara's laugh rippled through the quiet forest. "I just *did it*, Emerald. There's no how. You could do it if you believed you could."

"I don't think so," I said. "I would've figured it out by now."

"Nah," she told me. "People don't. They think magic—if that's what you want to call it—they think it's for books and stories. They never realize they're holding it in their hands." Zara stretched her legs out with mine, and they looked pretty together, as pretty as I'd hoped. "I like that," she said. "We match. It's kind of hot, too."

"I was picturing that," I admitted. "I was thinking how hot they would look next to each other? I don't know why it's so hot." I blushed then. It probably wasn't the right thing to say.

"They do look pretty." Zara wiggled her bare toes. "You wanna see something?"

"Uh, sure," I said, and she jumped to her feet. "We have to walk a little bit," she told me, pulling me up and bounding down the trail. "It's not far, though. You won't believe it. I saw it on the way here."

Zara held my hand, and she moved fast, a ground-covering stride that said she was used to hikes. Trumpet vines twined up cypress trunks; small birds flitted from branch to branch. The swamp was alive, summer-green, swelling and sprouting. "Are we going to your house?" I asked. "I'd love to see your place."

"Not my house," she said, but offered nothing else.

"You said you live near here, right?" She tugged me along, and I trotted to keep up. "What road?"

"Middle of nowhere," Zara told me promptly. "It's complicated. It's not my house."

She must've been staying with someone. Maybe it embarrassed her. I wouldn't want to bring Zara to my house, so I understood that. She'd see the sagged siding, the dirty walls, the unmown grass. Taken together, the battered house and beat-down cars looked more like laziness than poverty, but we couldn't help it. Time and energy were in short supply at my house. We didn't have a lawnmower, and the landlord didn't give a shit about snakes in the front yard; if you don't have a washer and dryer, dirty clothes pile up—laundromats are sad places, all meth heads and old ladies with trembling lips. The first will steal your quarters.

The second will moan about their grandchildren never visiting and late social security checks. Laundromats are a concentration of human misery, like the WIC office, all people life left behind. You wouldn't go there if you had a choice, and we put it off as long as possible. Our kitchen needed a scrub-down; eventually, Mama would holler at Jett to clean the bathroom. I'd help him scrape caked-up mold from the tiles. Our house reeked of good enough, of tired and tired of. Zara didn't need to see it. Maybe her house was the same way.

Zara stopped at a stream, wide and mazy. Curving through the cypress-forest like a sleepy country highway, it could've sheltered anything—alligator, catfish, gar as long as my leg. "We need to cross this creek," she said, hiking her dress to her thighs. Her tats were beautiful then, black on her brown skin, and a little thrill bubbled in my tummy. Mine probably looked just as good.

"Is it deep?" I eyed the molasses-slow water, black with tannin. I couldn't see the bottom.

"Nah. Nothing in there will bother you, either, so don't go all squicky on me." Her smile bloomed like a sunrise, and she stepped in. Nose wrinkled, I splashed after her. Dark water splashed my short-shorts. I followed close behind her, careful not to step in any holes. I didn't want to get wet, but the water was blessedly cool, and once I waded in, I resisted sinking down to my neck. I could've stayed in that stream all day. If I'd have lingered, floated on my back and watched the branches arching above, the water would whisper secrets in my ears. It would hold me like my grandmother's hugs, welcomed me, like it had waited for me to wade in.

Zara slipped up the bank and ducked behind a bush. "It's right up there," she whispered. "You have to be very quiet. He knows me, but he'll fly away from you." She pointed. Around an upstream bend, an egret picked through the shallows. White-plumed, yellow-legged, he peered at the water like he was reading a book. I drew a sharp breath. I'd never seen one so big.

"How can you know an egret?" I asked.

"Shh," she hissed.

The enormous bird picked through the shallows. All tensile strength, he stabbed into the water, came up with a fish, and took it down like a sword-swallower. I gasped.

"Hush," Zara told me. "If you're quiet, he'll stick around."

And he did. We crouched, silent, for almost half an hour as he poked through that creek.

After three more fish, he shrugged water from his feathers, kicked off the bottom, and flew soundlessly downstream.

"He was beautiful," I told Zara. In his silent wake, speaking seemed sacrilegious, like a cuss word in church.

Zara gazed after him. "The Indians here, before white people came, they kept tame cranes. Did you know that? The cranes flew away when smallpox came, and the people died so quick no one could bury them. Their bodies sank into the swamp." She drew a long, shuddery breath. "They were famous for their cranes. They wandered the village like pets. They're gone now. All of it's gone. We lost so much." She turned to me, expression fierce. "You have no idea, Emerald. None. Can you imagine the quiet? Happy quiet, people living with the land and the land living with them." She pronounced a word I didn't understand.

"What was that?" I asked, straightening up. My back had crinked. The swamp returned to its usual chorus, or maybe I just noticed it again.

She pronounced the word again. "It was their word that meant 'living together with the land.'"

"You mean from the Congaree Indians?" I asked. "When we learned about them in sixth grade, they said their language was gone."

Zara strode back to the stream and clambered down the bank. She used the cypress knees like stepping stones. "They were wrong," she told me, "and don't call them 'Congaree.' That was what the Catawba called them, not what they called themselves."

I wanted to ask what name they used. But Zara's mouth had hardened to a thin white line, and I didn't want to poke that anger. "What'd I do?" I asked, all caution.

"Nothing." She dropped into the stream, everything but her head underwater. "Sorry. I get mad about the Indians, y'know? A whole culture gone. No one thinks about them anymore."

I sank into the stream. That water held me like a whispered mercy. I closed my eyes and floated. Maybe I should've been afraid. People said there were cottonmouths thick as a thigh in that swamp, gators like compact cars, catfish the size of VW Bugs—they're always the size of VW Bugs; ask anyone for a big-fish catfish story, and they'll use that exact phrase. I don't know if they're really that huge, or if it's just a thing people say. I always wondered. So I should've been scared to float in that water. But it felt kind. *The stream won't let anything hurt me*, I thought, which was stupid, but there you go.

So we swam, soaking our clothes. Zara told me more about the Indians then. "How d'you know all this?" I asked.

"I just do," she told me, then talked about their skill with a spear. I listened. That was all she wanted, maybe—a witness, a listener, someone to shoulder their story and gather that sadness close. I understood that. So many times, I craved that understanding. When bad things happen, you want someone to see your hurt; lonely sadness is the worst kind. When kids laughed at my knock-off shoes, when they poked fun at my free lunches, when they called my family low-life trash, Mama would say, "Ignore them. They're jealous." *Of what*, I'd want to ask. *Nobody's jealous of being poor.* Only Alyssa would listen, and she didn't have a lot of patience for it. "Look on the good side, Emmy," she'd say. "Least you got sneakers and lunch. Plenty of people, they don't." *So where are they?* I'd want to say. *'Cause there sure as hell aren't many people in Lower Congaree poorer than me.*

So I listened to Zara. The swamp seemed to sing a counterpart to her words, and even the cypresses felt sadder, grayer, like they'd lost something they could never find again. Some of those trees were old enough to have seen those forgotten Indians. When Zara cried, I waded over and hugged her. Her head rested on my shoulder, and her tears smeared my neck. I wanted to tell her it was okay. I couldn't. It would never be okay. Something beautiful was gone forever.

When her tears went down to sniffles, she lifted her head. "I should get going," she told me.

"How can I get in touch with you?" I asked. "I mean, once I go home. We could text."

"I'll see you tomorrow," she said, scrambling up the bank. Mud smeared her pretty tattoos, but she didn't bother to wipe it off. "Can you come tomorrow? I promise not to be so sad. I'll show you something else. You'll like it. Swear."

"Yeah," I said. "I can come tomorrow." Either Zara didn't want to talk to me outside the swamp, or she wasn't ready. I had to be patient, maybe. People at home probably didn't know she liked girls.

"I'll see you then," she told me. "You know the way back?"

"Same time, same place?" I said. "Except—well—" I chose my words carefully, 'cause I didn't want her to think I was ashamed. "They don't know I come out here. My mama tells me not to, and she gets mad if she catches me. Is there anywhere else—"

"Yeah," she said. "You can drive, right? Drive to that place all the kids go to make out and take the north trail. I'll meet you about a mile in, at the stream bend." And she bounded away, that same quick stride.

When I reached home, I walked in the front door instead of the back. Mama was already making Sunday dinner, spaghetti and store-bought meatballs. Frozen ones were cheaper than hamburger meat. "Hey," I said to her and Jett. "My friend Amber and I went to the swimming hole. How was church?"

Mama fixed a beady eye on me. "Why didn't you take a goddamn bathing suit? Get in there and change. You're dripping all over the floor, Emmy Ann."

Ducking into the bedroom, I hid a secret smile. They had no idea.

In the morning, I drove to the Lot and hiked out. Mosquitoes had stopped bothering me; I didn't know if they weren't biting or I was used to them. Zara and I hugged when we met, then she bounced down the trail. "C'mon," she urged. "The surprise isn't far."

But it was, about three miles of far, but I didn't complain. Finally, she led me off the trail and slipped behind a bush. "Be really, really quiet," she said when I dropped next to her. "No one knows these are back here, and *you can't tell anyone*, Emerald. Swear."

"I swear," I told her solemnly, and hooked my pinkie into hers.

"Why'd you do that?" In the deep shade, she stared at our linked pinkies like I'd done something strange.

"Pinkie swear," I said, studying her wrinkled nose and creased forehead. Zara had the cutest confused face. "Didn't you pinkie swear when you were a kid?"

"Nah." She pointed to a craggy dead tree. "Now hush. It'll come back in a second."

Five minutes later, a bird landed on a splintery branch. Red-headed, black-bodied, it reminded me of those old Woody Woodpecker cartoons. I'd never seen anything like it; the bird was as big as a crow, bright-eyed. Brambles brushed my face as I crept closer.

"Ivory-billed woodpecker," Zara whispered.

"They're extinct!" I hissed.

"So everyone thinks." She flashed a wicked grin. Tears pricked my eyes. Not lost at all, but the swamp's best secret.

On Tuesday, Zara showed me the oldest cypress in the state. "It's older than Shakespeare," she said, and one more time, I almost cried. Instead, I rested my palm on its smooth bark. *Hello*, I said to it. *Thank you for still being here.*

A flush of love overwhelmed me, sure as my gramma's hug. Zara rested her head against its rough trunk. "Think of the stories it has," she said.

"I wish I could hear them." I stroked its bark, cracked as mud parched by sunshine.

Zara touched my cheek. "Maybe you'll hear them someday," she told me, and it didn't feel crazy, but sweet.

On Wednesday, my eyes popped, and I cowered in the brush as an albino gator heaved from the muck. It really was as big as a compact car, a swamp-giant, white and red-eyed and strange. "He won't hurt you," Zara whispered. "He's blind, and he doesn't like to leave the water."

When the gator sank again, I bolted. Brush crashed; birds shouted; legs pumping, I ran like the devil was chasing me. Mud splashed my thighs as I crashed through puddles. Smilax scratching my calves, trumpet vine whipping my face, I ran til I gasped and finally reached the path. Cypresses and woodpeckers were one thing, and enormous gators were another. When Zara caught up, she was laughing. "He wouldn't hurt you," she told me.

"I'd rather not take my chances," I said.

Zara dropped against a fallen log. And held out her arms. "C'mere," she told me, and we stretched out on the pillowy moss.

"Thank you for sharing this with me," she said.

Our foreheads touched. We were gonna kiss again, really kiss for the first time in days, and a sweet need tugged between my legs. "Thank you for showing me all this."

Zara pulled me closer. Her thigh parted mine, and she kissed me. It was another of those delicious slow kisses, gentle, like she was trying to figure me out with her lips. I rested a palm on her cheek. I'd dreamed of this softness, soft skin and soft bodies, all curves melting into each other. "You feel so good," Zara said against my lips.

"You too," I whispered. The whole forest seemed to hold us, and we were alone with it. Our kiss rose into something wild and perfect, like a lightning storm or a driving rain. Zara's hand slid between us. She thumbed my nipple through my tank top, and I pressed against her thigh. She pushed it higher. When I cupped her breast, she gasped. Zara wasn't wearing a bra, and her nipples were button-hard.

"Here." She scooted back. "Take off your clothes. Please? I want to feel you against me."

A few days ago, I would've blushed. I would've made an excuse, something dumb, but life had shifted in ways I never imagined, and I shucked off everything. Zara lifted her dress. When she flipped on top of me, her warm pussy pressed mine. We kissed, and I couldn't think, 'cause her hips were rocking, and my clit slid against her. I thought girls rubbing against each other was a porn thing, like they did it for guys, but that sweet pressure made me bite my lip. I was getting wet, opening up, and Zara was slippery against me. When she lifted up a bit and quickly spread us both, I couldn't help but gasp. I swear I felt her clit, like a tiny, plump little nub.

I whimpered when she moved away, but her hand moved between my legs. When a slim finger slipped inside me, she pressed a place inside me guys could never find, and her thumb brushed my clit. Barely grazing me, she petted like I was delicate and special. No one had ever been so gentle. I couldn't help wiggling my hips.

I dared to slip a palm between her legs. Her pussy was silky-soft, and her lips were delicate, like flowers, those thin, frilled edges. When I slid a finger into her, she purred and spread her legs. I didn't quite know how to touch her, so I moved my thumb like she did, barely skimming her, like I'd stroke a newborn kitten. I snuggled closer. Zara stopped for a moment to shed her dress. Before she settled next to me again, I only grabbed a quick peek, but her nipples were tight and red. I must have pinched them hard. Her skin was such a pretty brown, and I didn't think they would be pink.

But her thumb slipped back to my clit, and I stopped thinking. We were curled close together, stretched on our backs. The swamp seemed to breathe with us. We were together in it, cradled in the forest's dark, secret heart. I smelled warm earth, wind in the trees, the sharp scent of water. Time stretched like a lazy cat. That perfect tension built, and Zara's thumb never sped up.

When her breath came quicker, I realized she was as close as me. I arched my hips up. Zara made a small, sweet sound, and her pussy tightened, tightened, tightened. She seemed to quiver there, motionless, then both of us broke like a wave in the same shattering moment. Maybe we gasped or pressed closer or bucked our hips. I was lost in it. I never thought it could be like that. I never believed it, or believed in it. Sex always felt like racing myself to a finish. But we were two people alone with the trees and earth and shimmering green, and we were beautiful.

Eventually, our hands moved. Still as forest creatures, we cuddled together on that moss. "I'm scared to talk, 'cause I don't want to ruin it," Zara whispered.

"Me too." She smelled warm, like herself, like everything I ever wanted.

Quiet, we stayed that way for a long time. She was warm, cushiony instead of hard-edged. I never wanted to leave. But we had to sit up eventually. We had to get up, and we had to join the world again. When Zara shifted back, I opened my eyes.

Her nipples were still red. I didn't think I pinched them that hard. I bit back a gasp when I realized they weren't nipples at all, but berries, red and bright, like holly or sumac. Hard, nubby little things, they stood stiff. I scrambled backward and hit rough cypress bark. Under my thumb, her clit had felt like that. And between her legs—those delicate lips—I leapt up and stared.

Zara squinched her eyes shut.

I stammered something, all nonsense. My heart kicked up.

"It's not what you think," Zara said, and her arms went around her chest. "Emerald, just listen for a second."

"You felt like flower petals," I managed.

"Please." Zara dropped her head, and her dark hair fell in her face, like she wanted to hide from me. I knew that feeling. It would've ached if I wasn't so scared. "I'm so lonely. You understand that. You could stay here with me, if you wanted to. We can be together here forever and always, Emerald."

"What are you?" That realization came slowly, then all at once. Zara couldn't do magic. She *was* magic. I thought fairy tales weren't real. I thought there was nothing past what I could touch, a long, blank, endless nothing. I didn't know which was scarier.

Zara seemed so small, no clothes on, hunched next to that fallen log. "I just want to be with you," she said. "We'll never be lonely. We can take care of each other and be in love and be happy. I want to wake up next to you in the morning, Emerald."

"No." I was hugging myself, too. We were naked in the forest, far apart.

"Emerald." Zara grabbed my arm, and I jerked away. "Please. I waited for you. You always went on walks, and I saw you, and I finally got up enough courage to talk to you—"

"You *watched me?*" I didn't know fear had a taste. But it does, like blood and pennies, sharp and bitter. I snatched my clothes and held them in front of me.

"Please don't go." Her eyes filled. "Please stay with me, at least for a little while if you don't want to stay for always—"

"No." I clutched my clothes to my chest.

"Please. You hate those people because they don't accept you." Zara drew her knees up to her chest. "I just want the—"

I held my clothes in front of me, and I ran. I leapt roots. Mud splashed up my legs and hid those pretty tattoos. She wasn't a person. She was something else entirely.

"Emerald!" Zara shouted, already far away.

I didn't look back.

Back in my car, I floored it. It's strange how you think something as flimsy as a door can save you. It's hope more than belief. Maybe that hope's so strong it holds those bad things on the other side of the door, driving them back with nothing more than wishes. I could've believed it. I could've believed a lot of things then.

"What's wrong?" Jett called when I slammed inside and ducked in my room. Luckily, no one else was home. "Emmy? You okay?"

"Fine!" I shouted back. *I hooked up with something that isn't human.*

"You just seemed really, uh, freaked." He sounded far away, like the house had warped and stretched between us.

"No, I'm good!" I buried my head in my pillow. Halfway down the path, I'd stopped and pulled my clothes on. I wanted to strip them off and shower, like I could wash off all that fear. Zara wasn't human. I had no place to slot her or name to call her.

Tired from running and other things I didn't want to think about, I fell asleep. If you'd have asked, I'd have told you I was too scared to sleep, but I passed out anyway. Maybe I was so terrified that my body shut down rather than face whatever waited in that swamp.

When I woke up, the sun was setting in pinks and golds. Dirty laundry humped up in piles. At the bottom of my bed, an old patchwork quilt tangled with sheets, a blanket, my old teddy bear. Once I was a little girl. Once I'd believed in fairy tales but then I grew up and decided they were a dream. I walked in the swamp 'cause I thought nothing could touch me. I shoved up and stripped off my clothes. New ones felt a little bit better.

When I went in the kitchen, Mama didn't turn from the stove. In that harsh white light, all her grays showed, and she looked like an old woman, hunchback and tired. "Sit your ass down," she snapped. "You tell me where the hell you were all day."

She hadn't seen me leave. Had she seen me come home? Her question had no right answer. Mama was good at those. I wondered if it was her, or if all mothers had that talent.

"I told you to sit down, Emmy Ann," Mama said.

That name—that was a little girl's name. After what I saw in that swamp, I wasn't a little girl anymore. "Emerald." My voice didn't waver. "My name is Emerald."

"You think I don't know that when I gave it to you?" She gestured with her wooden spoon like she was holding a sword. "Sit your ass down. You and I need to have a conversation."

The day was bad enough. I wouldn't add a lecture from Mama on top of it. I'd seen a person who wasn't a person at all, and beside that, standing up to Mama felt like nothing. Why would she scare me? She was human. "No," I told her. "You're gonna yell at me for something. I'm twenty-one years old. You can talk like I'm an adult, but you aren't gonna sit me down and shout like I'm ten."

Mama studied me for a moment. "Sit down," she told me.

That anger coiled up again. It tangled in my chest and climbed my throat, and I thought for a moment I'd strangle. Everyone thought I'd shut up and do what I was told. "No," I said again.

Mama was gonna lose it—when she was real mad, she'd shout something like, *You don't talk to your mother like that. You respect your elders, you hear me, Emmy Ann? I brought you into this world and I can take you out of it.*

"You were in that swamp again." Mama spoke it like a statement, not a question, and I knew I was in real trouble, more than I'd ever been before.

"So what if I was?" I wanted to plant my back against that sorry-ass kitchen wall. I would've felt those familiar nicks and scratches bump under my hand, and they'd have felt something like safe. But stepping back would look weak, and I was too mad for weak. I was grown. I had a job and my own choices and damn if she'd tell me different.

The evening light drew her in sharp, hard shadows. It showed her wrinkles. Mama looked like a storybook witch, like she'd lived long and lived hard, all gray roots and gnarled fingers. "You don't go in that swamp. I told you and told you and damn if you ever listen to me, Emmy Ann!"

"I told you, my name is Emerald," I said.

"Whatever the fuck you wanna call yourself!" Her spoon hit the counter like God's own judgment.

I looked at that spoon. I looked at her. A lifetime in the chicken plant had shriveled her up, like it sucked down her insides and left her hollowed-out. That made me almost as angry as her yelling. Life had beaten her down before she had a chance. "I went in that swamp 'cause I wanted to," I said. "I heard what you said. But I made my own choices."

"What the hell d'you even mean?" she snapped. "What the fuck d'you do out there, Emmy Ann?"

I couldn't hide anymore. She could like it or not like it, but I was tired of lying. I could've pretended I wasn't out there with Zara. For a moment, I thought about it. But lying would've meant denying who I was. I stood in that tiny kitchen next to the battered table where I'd done my homework, and my toes curled into the rag rug my gramma made. I'd lied there so many times. I was Emerald, and I was done with it.

"I went out there to meet a girl," I said. "I like girls. I mean, like I'm bisexual. You can like it or not, but that's who I am."

Diamond must've overheard us shouting and heaved herself off the couch. Her moon-face appeared in the doorway, and she was grinning. I wanted to smack that smile off her face. From the kitchen table, Jett and Aunt Tabby stared. The moment held and held, silent, tearing.

Mama finally spoke. "What are you saying, Emerald Ann Joiner?"

"I said I like girls." I spoke loudly, like I had nothing to be ashamed of. And there was nothing shameful about it. If there was shame, they handed it to me. I could refuse it. I would never wear anyone else's shame again—not for liking girls, not for my job, and not for being a Joiner, either.

"You like girls." Mama spoke in that same cool voice again, the dangerous one. "You know what people in this town will say about me if they find out you're running around with women?"

"My choices are mine." I balled my fists and I believed it. That anger burst into full flower. I was myself. "Who I am has nothing to do with you, and I won't change it 'cause you're afraid of what people will say."

Don't, my brother mouthed. *Stop it.*

They could accept me or not. Zara accepted me. Something in my chest slid sideways. Zara wasn't human. "I won't stop it," I said. "I am who I am and I'm not apologizing anymore."

"Then you can get your fancy self outta this house," Mama replied, and my aunt nodded along with her. "I'm sick and tired of your bullshit. I won't have you running around this town tattooed up like a whore and saying you're one of those lesbos. You're not that way. I raised you better than that."

She gripped the counter behind her like she was clinging to a ledge, ready to tumble over, and holding on was her last best hope. Below her shorts, her feet were bare. Those bare feet with pink-painted toes almost broke my heart. They seemed so vulnerable, the saddest part of her. But anger crumpled her face, and she meant every word.

Mama and Aunt Tabby, Diamond and Jett, they all watched me. We were five strangers in that little room, people crammed together by accidents of birth. That house was like a bus station. We moved in and out of it, never staying, always glancing warily at one another. It would be like that until someone agreed to change it. They wouldn't try, or they didn't know how, and one person couldn't do it alone.

"You want me to leave?" I asked. "Then I'll leave. You can kick me out like you kicked out Jackson. You don't love us anymore 'cause we're doing the best we can? Then you can fuck right off, Mama. I'm done with you." Back straight, I walked outta that kitchen like I was striding a catwalk.

"What the hell was that?" Aunt Tabby shouted behind me. "You respect your mama, y'hear me?"

I ignored her.

I could've flung myself on that bed and cried. I could've run back there and begged. The girl I loved wasn't a girl at all, and Mama had kicked me out of the house for nothing more than being myself. I might've lost it.

I grabbed a duffle bag and packed. Last of all, I grabbed my cash, hidden in an old backpack under my bed—every week, I stopped at the bank, and I deposited all the money Mama didn't take, and Jett and I didn't need—usually only fifty bucks or so, and that ran out quick. Glaring, the tellers touched my money like it would make them sick. They knew where it came from. But I was done caring about that.

I wasn't scheduled to work that night. I didn't much care. I had nowhere else to go.

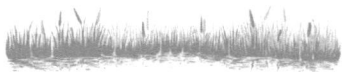

"Hey, Luna!" Noah called as I walked into the club's weird twilight. "I didn't think you were on tonight!"

"I'm not." I leaned against the bar. "I thought I'd come in anyway. Not much to do at home." Not like I had a home, or a girlfriend—if I'd ever had a girlfriend. While we curled in that swamp and kissed each other, I thought I did. That hurt more than Mama. Fear was eroding into sadness. I couldn't love someone who wasn't human. *She's not a someone,* I told myself. *She's something else entirely.*

"Well, head on back." Noah grabbed a Coke and slid it down the bar. "Anyone bothers you, lemme know."

Back in the dressing room, I didn't tell Alyssa why Mama kicked me out, but she said I could stay with her for a little while. I was glad about that. Least I knew where I'd lay my head. "Imma head home 'bout midnight," she told me. "Lucky's daddy says he has to work in the morning, and he can't stay longer than that." She swooped me into a hug. Alyssa smelled like roses, and I wished for Zara's honeysuckle. "I'm so sorry, Emmy," she told me.

"Thanks," I said, and it should've made me feel better. Alyssa and I had been besties since we were five. It didn't matter. She didn't know anything about me.

I slipped into Luna. When you need money, you do what you have to, even if life is crumbling to pieces. The guys distracted me. They wrapped their arms around my waist and breathed into my ear. I tried not to wish they were Zara. Rubbing on those guys, I stepped through dance after dance, but I gave myself one heartsick indulgence. "Hey," I said to the DJ, "do Nine Inch Nails's 'Sunspot' for me next, will you?"

"Cool," he replied, half-zoned, already high on something. Maybe you'd have to be.

I stalked onstage in those fat platform heels. I wore black and chains and a leather collar; men watched me from the dark beyond the stage lights. The song was slow, and I worked it, shook my ass, climbed that pole, dropped my top and grabbed my tits. I mouthed words, and music thrummed through me. I was part of that throbbing beat, everything I wanted and could never have. Eyes begging me to stay, Zara had been so sad. She wasn't a person, but maybe I'd run too soon. Maybe I should've listened, even if I was scared. The music filled me up, and I held it against the day's raw misery. All those men, those people watching, they made me into Emmy Joiner, just like my mother had. I would never be anything else for them. I tried not to look in their eyes but they stared. I was naked, and they thought they knew me.

My vines were beautiful under the lights, dark, marking me as something wild and unknowable and strange. They were mine. Zara had put them there, but I wanted them. *Who are you, Emerald Joiner?* someone might've asked, and I'd have pointed to those tattoos. *I'm that*, I'd have told them. *That's me, right there, take it or leave it.* I could've broken down. I let the music take me instead.

When I stepped off that stage, I found three twenties tucked in my thong. It was money. It meant nothing. They wanted something, but it wasn't me.

"That was amazing, Luna," Noah said when I hit the bar.

"Thanks." I swiped at my face and drained my Coke. I wouldn't think about Mama. I wouldn't think about Zara.

"Car still running okay?" he asked.

"Sure," I said.

"Lemme know if you ever need anything," he told me. "I'm always here to help you out, you know that, right?"

"Hey, girl." Alyssa touched my shoulder. She was wearing street clothes. "I'm headed home, okay? Key's under the doormat."

"Thanks." I got up and hugged her. One more time, I wished for Zara. No one at that club knew me. They might've called me Luna, but I was Emmy Ann there, one more poor girl scrambling to catch whatever leftovers other people tossed away. Alyssa opened the door to a dark night, a glimpse of stars, then shut it behind her. Girls sat on laps. Hazy in the cigarette smoke, they seemed soft-edged, blurred, like men could mold them into daydreams. I was one of them. When I picked up my Coke, Noah was studying me.

"You and Alyssa partying after work?" He smiled a little. "Do I get an invite?"

Noah knew I lived with Mama and Aunt Tabby, but it was the kind of thing you overlooked, like someone's bad breath or underarm sweat. And he'd find out I left—the club ran on rumor and gossip and catty backbiting. "My mom kicked me out," I said. "I'm staying with Alyssa for a while."

He set down his rag and rested his elbows on the bar. "So your mama made you leave?"

I hadn't thought about blurring the truth, and I cussed myself. I could've said I moved out. "Yeah, she did," I said. "She finally lost it about my dancing, I guess."

"Really?" he asked. "You've been dancing for six months."

I could tell him or not tell him. No one knew me, and maybe it was time they did. I was tired of being Emmy Joiner, and Luna, all those masks I kept between me and the outside world. It was time to take them off. "Yeah," I said. "But she found out I like girls, and that put her over the edge."

I didn't blush. I didn't stutter, or look down, or hide behind my hair. Instead, I watched Noah's face cloud into something like confusion. "You like girls?" he asked. "What d'you mean?"

I drained my Coke. "I mean I'm bi, and I'd rather be with girls." The music seemed far away, and my words were too real for that Christmas light glow.

"You're like that?" Noah's expression changed, but I couldn't read it, good or bad.

"Yeah," I said, 'cause I couldn't back down then.

"Huh." It could've meant anything. Dread brooded in my belly.

"Imma go dance," I said. "I'll let you know when I need walked out." I left him there at the bar. Maybe I shouldn't have told him, but I was tired of it. I'd left Zara and Mama. I'd lost all my choices, and the world cleared into bare bones. That happens when you have nothing else to lose. You go all-in 'cause there's nothing else left.

I smoked and drank and laughed. I worked tables of guys. Maybe they liked me not caring what they thought. It made me untouchable somehow. "You wanna go out back?" one asked, arm tightening around me.

"Not really, no," I told him instead of giggling.

He blushed, and then bought three dances. "Your tats are amazing," he said when it was over.

"Thanks," I replied, straightening up.

"I wish..." His eyes were sad, like Zara's, and he stopped. Once I would have giggled, or maybe asked what he wished for, but I walked away instead.

Noah passed me drinks when I hit the bar, but he didn't say much. He was distant and I finally saw it: That distance said something about him, not me. When Mama flew off the handle, it wasn't my fault. She was fed-up with an idea she'd created, and I had very little to do with it.

The club seemed so small then. It was all a set-up. Men came in, and we gave them a night of fairy tales. It didn't last. They would go back to their gritty, sweaty jobs, their worried nights, the women they didn't like who didn't like them. Usually I thought about handing them dreams, and it made me sort of happy. I could give them something, and it might make life a little better, a little more bearable. But it didn't matter, not in the end. It would never get better for those men. They'd slave away til they died or got too hurt to work anymore. Old men, bitter, I imagined them sitting on porches, counting time-rotted dreams. They'd hope in Jesus and the lottery. Neither would come through. I saw their whole lives, from their unwanted beginnings to their lonely, sputtering deaths, and I could've run outta that club crying. They were drowning men, clutching life's soaked remnants. They'd sink in the end.

Men gathered their cigarettes and paid their bar tabs and drove into the night. I changed into shorts and a tank top. When I appeared at the bar, the house lights were up. The sticky floor shone; empty glasses and balled-up cocktail napkins scattered the tables. Its party had moved on; real life had swooped in and blown away the dream. "You mind walking me out?" I asked Noah.

"No." He stopped counting bottles and came around the bar. "I wanted to talk to you anyway. C'mon."

I should've smiled. There was nothing that should've worried me, but I worried anyway. Something wasn't right. I held my bag tight as we passed through the door and into the parking lot. Noah stopped as we rounded the corner. The lot was dark, but the trees beyond were darker. Night seemed to snag and linger in them. Normally, it might've scared me, but that darkness felt like an old friend.

"Listen, Luna." Noah ruffled his hair. "I'm worried about you."

I'd had enough of people worried about me. I might've relaxed, but he'd offered something, and I knew what he was thinking. "I'm fine," I told him. "Really. I'm staying at Alyssa's, and I'll save enough for my own place in a few—"

Noah stepped closer. He tucked a strand of hair behind my ear, and I went as still as a hunted creature in that humming swamp. "You can stay with me."

"Thank you," I said carefully. "But I'm good at Alyssa's. It's really kind of you to—"

"Emmy." Noah was watching me, not that night-forest. "Your car's half-dead and you don't have anywhere to go. You can stay with me, honey." He was too close, his breath in my face. It smelled like cherry Lifesavers. Strange, the things you grab when you're panicking, those sensations that hit hard and won't leave. "You don't need to stay with Alyssa."

His eyes reminded me of the men watching beside the stage, the greedy ones that saw something and wanted it. Cicadas thrummed, and something rustled in those leaning trees. On most nights, those sounds would have sent me shivering. Instead, they seemed to feed some deep-down bravery.

"I'm good with Alyssa," I told him. My voice stayed cautious. The humidity clung to my back, and it seemed too hot for darkness.

Noah's shoulders sagged. Hunched into himself, a bird in the rain, he drew back. "You and Alyssa have a thing, don't you?"

"No," I said. "Why would you think that? She has Lucky, and—"

"I've been trying." His voice was small against the swamp sounds, so dim it almost drowned in cicada-hum. "Y'know, I've tried so hard, Emmy. I did everything but tell you straight out. I never asked for anything—I know how those guys inside are. I don't wanna be like them."

"You're not," I assured him, reflexively, like it was my job to make him feel better. "There's nothing with Alyssa and me—we've been friends since kindergarten. But—Noah—" I drew a shuddery breath. "You're my boss." Mama would've told me, *Don't shit where you eat*, and that was an ugly way to say it, but she was right.

Girls like me had to be careful. A man with power over us would only snatch more.

"Is that all?" Noah straightened. Uncurling, he took my hands in his. I managed not to flinch back. "Emmy, that doesn't matter. I'd be so good to you. If it's the thing with girls—listen, you think you like girls, but you're confused. You need someone to keep you safe, keep you away from all this. You shouldn't be in that club."

Gently, I pulled back. Untamed, quietly savage, the swamp loomed around us, like it might creep closer and swallow us both. Normally, I would've shivered. But it felt as familiar as a soft blanket. "It's not just that," I said carefully. "I like you. I do. And if things were different—" I struggled. He was kind, and I hated hurting him. "I don't like many guys, Noah. Not at all."

He pressed his lips together and glanced at the swamp, then shivered. "Did someone scare you, Emmy? That happens to girls sometimes, scares them away from men. It's not like that. I can show you."

I ached. Noah was like everyone in that town, small-minded, stuffing me into slots I'd never fit. "No one hurt me," I said, and those trees, their leaning branches, the dripping moss and wilding brush, they lent me a strength I'd never had. Green and growing, it roiled like a brushfire in my chest. "This is me—this is who I am. I'm sorry."

Drawing his elbows close, Noah kicked at the dirt. "Of fucking course. I end up liking the girl who wants another girl. Something like this always happens, y'know? I do my goddamn best. I try so hard not to be like those other guys. Maybe I should be. That's what girls want, isn't it?"

"It's not what I want," I told him.

"Of-fucking-course-not, 'cause you think you want pussy instead. You don't. You'll figure it out." His expression twisted into meanness. "You'll figure it out, Emmy, and I'll be gone. Don't ask me again. I'm done with you." Jaw clenched, Noah kicked another dusky-dry puff of dust. Gravel grated as he stomped back to the club. I could've collapsed. Goddamn him. Goddamn all those men who thought women owed them something. I hefted my bag and strode to my car. With my luck, it wouldn't start. I'd have to ask him for help, and he'd leave me there—

A hand closed over my wrist, and I bit back a scream. Noah wasn't done. But when I whirled, Isaac Wheeler leered at me. Fear clotted my throat, sharp and bitter-black.

"I been waiting for you, Emmy Joiner," he said.

"I told you no." Cicada-shrieks soared to a deafening thrum. That swamp was meaner, closer. You could lose yourself in it—lose yourself and never come back. It should've scared me.

"And I offered you good money." Isaac's breath reeked of stale beer and cigarettes. "I offered you three hundred and fifty, girl. You think you're too good for me? I know you fuck around. The whole town knows it."

"I don't." When I tried to back away, his grip tightened. He knew what he was gonna do. Isaac had already made a decision; he'd come to that dark parking lot and waited.

"This can go easy or it can go real bad." He yanked me closer. I cringed back. Isaac was already hard, and maybe that frightened me worst: He got off on scaring me. When he grabbed my hair and forced my head back, I knew I was fucked. Isaac pushed his tongue in my mouth, and I almost gagged from the rotten taste. I wouldn't open my teeth, and his thin tongue licked my lips.

"What the *fuck*?" someone shouted, and Isaac jerked back.

"Just some fun," he snapped. "What's—"

A fist flashed, and I flew back as his nose crunched with a shuddering, audible crack.

"I told you I'd beat your ass if you touched her!" Noah shouted. Isaac was down, and Noah kicked his gut, his crotch. Isaac screamed as his fingers broke under Noah's boot. When Noah booted his stomach, a soft squeak slipped from him. You'd think a beat-down like that would be loud, but it wasn't. Noah's foot thumped on flesh; Isaac let out little whimpers. Soon he was curled up and crying, and Noah spit in his face.

"Get the fuck outta here," he said. "If I ever see you again, I'll kill you."

Isaac scrambled up and ran.

"Hey, Emmy." Noah swooped me into his arms. I'd frozen, watching him, unable to look away. "Hey," he said, rocking me back and forth. "You're safe. You're safe now. I was so worried something like this would happen to you. I told you, this is no place for a girl like you."

I was too scared to cry. Noah smelled like Old Spice and cherry Lifesavers. "You're okay, you're safe," he murmured over and over. Relieved, I melted into him. My heart beat like a panicked bird, fluttering, trying to escape. I took deep breaths. It was almost working until I realized Noah's lips were against my neck.

"You taste good," he whispered.

"This isn't—" I started.

"Shhh." He kissed my neck, then moved up to my ear. "Shh, Emmy," he said over the swamp's night-songs. "Shh, honey. This is how it's supposed to be. See how good this is?"

"Let go," I told him, and when I struggled, he hugged me tighter. That fear rose again, sharp-tasting and bright. "Stop it."

"This can be so nice," Noah said, and his dick pressed my stomach. He arched his hips into me, and nausea rolled somewhere in my midsection. "See how nice this is?" His mouth came down on mine.

No one was gonna touch me again. No one was gonna tell me who I was and what I wanted. I wrenched back and broke loose. Almost amazed at my own strength, I paused for one slivered moment. Noah snatched at me. My hands went around his neck, and I squeezed tight.

I shouldn't have been able to do it. I knew that as I felt his pulse flutter under my fingers. But all that anger bubbled up—anger at Mama, anger at him, anger at that town determined to make me feel small. Everyone tried to tell me who I was and who I needed to be. I wouldn't let it happen anymore.

Eyes bulging, Noah dropped to his knees. Parking lot dust grated and puffed up, a dry smell, like hungry earth. The swamp hummed louder, meaner, as angry as me. My hands squeezed tight as trumpet vine. What was I doing? I shouldn't do this. But something was roiling in me, green, vicious, wicked and gleaming. My thumbs pressed deeper.

In that sweet, swallowing darkness, my arms were changing. Vines began at my fingertips and climbed upward, black, coiling, and a terrible strength infused me. Noah would never hurt anyone. He'd never hurt anyone else again. *Yes,* that swamp-chorus exalted. *Make him hurt. Make him pay for it.* Every cicada-hum stiffened my grip. Those shrieking tree frogs joined me, those birds, the towering trees and clinging vines. I felt the white alligator then. I felt the ivory-bills, and the small, creeping creatures, and the moon brooding on wind-rustled leaves. Black vines writhed up my arms, fingers to shoulder, down my chest and over my stomach. They met the tattoos on my legs and snaked downward. I was Emerald. Standing with my feet spread apart, all that strength bent into my hands, I knew what I was doing. Green overtook me, bloomed in me. As Noah's arms flailed, his hands clawed at mine. I squeezed harder. In the movies, death comes fast, but this wasn't fast at all. Noah's tongue stuck out, and his eyes rolled. He scrambled to stand but I held him down.

"You're not gonna tell me who I am," I told him.

He tried to speak but no words came out. His feet scrabbled at the dirt.

"I see who you are," I said. "You pretend to like me, but you just want something. You're exactly like the rest of them. You think you can tell me who to be?" My thumbs dug into him. "This is who I am, you bastard."

Noah's arms were going limp, and his hands had no strength left. He was gonna fall but if I let go I wouldn't finish it. His hand slapped my leg, my arms, those vines, dark on my pale skin. I was Emerald Joiner, and no one would ever hurt me again. Noah's good looks went ravaged and old. I saw him. He was like all the others, and I was finished with them.

Noah's eyes rolled back. When they closed, he flopped into my hands. My thumbs hurt, and I let go. Noah crumpled like a doll. He was gone, and something broke in me then. That green feeling shattered, and I was one person alone in a parking lot. I understood then why murderers stare at their hands. You can't believe you could do that. You look at a corpse and you look at your hands and you think, *There was a person and now there's not anymore. My hands did that.*

You'd think you'd panic. I didn't. I stood over that body and I made myself look at it. Noah was smaller dead than he'd looked alive, a little heap of a thing. The police would uncurl him. They'd say, *Who did this? Whose fingerprints are on his neck?* Then they'd find me.

And even if they didn't find me, or they did and I got out of it, I'd never escape, not really, not Noah or anyone else in that town. I'd always be Emmy Joiner, a broke-ass whore, nothing and no one to anybody. They didn't know me. They didn't want to. *Get out*, I imagined Alyssa saying. *I wouldn't have someone that perverted around Lucky. You always looked at me when we changed, didn't you?*

I could tell them who I was. They wouldn't care. They'd do their best to cram me into the box they made, and if I refused to fit, they'd force me. I stood in that dark parking lot and I knew it. Then I reached for the swamp and it was there, throbbing with life, with a glory I'd never imagined. Dazed, I stumbled to my car.

Zara would understand. She'd say, *You did the right thing. You didn't let him hurt you, and you stood up for who you are.*

In that close, panting dark, I felt vines twining my body. When I glanced down, the dark marks on my arms were still there. They were mine. I was with the swamp, and the swamp was with me.

Mama had shoved me in a box, like I wasn't a person at all. Like Zara. I'd treated Zara the same way. She'd never hurt me, and she could have. She could've kept me in that swamp forever and ever, even if I said no. My tattoos told me that. *You're not human*, I told her, like Mama said, *You're not that way*, or Noah told me, *You're not like that*. I tried to show them who I was, and they said, *No, you can't be that way. We'll change you if we have to*. Nothing could break the confines of their small lives. This town was full of jailers, and they kept themselves locked up.

Zara asked for understanding. She showed me who she was, and I said, *You're not human.* Was it any different, really? More misery settled down. No one needed to tell me the answer.

I could've ignored it. When it suits us, we ignore a lot of things. Brave people have the courage to look. I lived in a town full of cowards, but I didn't have to be one. If nothing else taught me that, my hands on Noah's neck had.

You hold on tight, Emmy Ann, Talitha told me. Around me, the swamp sang a hundred soaring songs. That strange power flowed through me again, different from me but not different at all. It was me. I had it all along. Zara had told me that. *You could do it if you believed you could.*

My car started, and I drove home, back to Mama's house. I knew what I had to do and where I had to go. That town would try to hold me, but I wouldn't let it. Those people would pin me down like one of those old-timey butterflies in a glass case. They would say, *This is Emmy Ann Joiner. This is who she is, and she will never escape it. You can't change who you are.*

I couldn't escape it, not there. I drove down that long, straight swamp highway, and wind played in my hair. Wet heat sucked at me; I might've hated it, but it felt like home. I thought of Mama's hands, their swollen joints and arthritic knuckles. She'd done the best she could. Everyone in this town did the best they could, and it was never enough. Life would break you. It would squeeze you dry and wring you out and leave you with nothing but your own empty hands. People like us Joiners, we'd never grab a toehold. The deck was stacked and the dice were loaded. We spent our days falling through empty air, nothing to catch us, no bottom to hit. It never changed. It never would.

I'll get my own place, I said. *I'll get an education.* I could've laughed as I threaded down those narrow roads, small cuts through deep swampland. Even if I managed to escape the body in that lonely parking lot, life would stay snatched-breath desperate, at my mama's house or my own, educated or not. Gravel grated as I pulled into the driveway, too loud over screaming cicadas and screechy tree frogs. I was done with the loneliness, the defeat, the you're-not-good-enough. I was Emerald, and I was finished.

I parked. My mother and brother, sister and aunt slept, wrapped in their own secret dreams. I'd never know them. They were their own people, misunderstood, maybe trying to do their best but busy holding one another down. Crabs in a bucket, Mama always said. I didn't know she was talking about herself.

High above, stars hung like promises; the moon was high and fat and round as an orange. When I stepped into the yard, tall grass brushed my calves. That warm swamp-smell hit my nose, standing water and deep mud, safe as it had always been. I walked around the trailer. There was my old window, and from the yard, I heard Diamond's familiar snoring. I wished I could talk to her. *We're sisters*, I'd have said. *We had differences but they don't matter, not really. I love you. I know you love me, deep down, behind all that sadness. You're trapped, and you want someone to blame.* She'd laugh, maybe cry, and stomp away. *You like girls,*

Emmy Ann, she'd say. *That's gross, and I don't want my baby around it.* That baby would grow up like her, small-minded in a small town. I ached for it. I hope she woke up and got out one day.

Cicada hum swelled like the symphonies I'd never heard. At the end of the path, I kicked off my sandals. I wouldn't need them anymore. I wouldn't need so many things. I'd walked past my mother's house and come home. When I passed under those sheltering cypresses, night scooped me into its arms. I would never be alone again.

"Emerald?" a soft voice called.

"I'm sorry," I told Zara. I didn't see her, but I felt her, a soft breeze on my cheek. "I shouldn't've run. I should've listened. You won't hurt me. And you deserve—" I struggled. "They try to put me in a box. I did the same to you."

A familiar hand slipped into mine. Cypresses hid the sky, and the dark was thick as a blanket, too thick for me to see. "You came back," Zara said. Her breath tickled my ear, humidity rising from a hundred little pools. "Will you stay for a little bit?"

"I'll stay as long as you want me," I told her. "There's nothing out there but meanness." I reached for her, but touched nothing. "It helped me." I whispered it like a confession, one of those things Catholics save for priests in stark black boxes. Zara would know what "it" meant. "I needed it, and it came."

"You understand now." A hand brushed my hair aside. I tilted my head to it, but it had gone, or it was never there. "It'll always be there for you, Emerald. I've been waiting."

Inside me, beauty burst to full flower. I was vivid, growing, strong as those vines. I didn't reach for Zara. I knew her. She was in the alligator, the ivory-bills, the streams and the trees and the dark-tannin water. The wind whispered hymns to her. Water babbled with love. As I melted into her, the strength of trees lifted me. Oh, she was lovely, dark, full of secrets. The ferocity of her night-black panther rooted around my heart. I was complete, free. I had become everything I dreamed.

"It'll always be awful out there," Zara told me, and her voice was a brush-rustle of loveliness. "They don't want anything different. C'mon, Emerald."

We were safe. I felt her, all of her, the long stretch of rich, green forest breathing with me. Swamp was an ugly word, short and fat, but Zara was bright in the darkness. We were together in that vine-tangled beauty, and her lips were soft as new-green grass. I knew hawks and otters then, deer and boars and that sleek panther, a whole wild world untouched and unimaginable.

I stepped inside.

Swamp Girl

I watch everyone who comes into the forest, and I hate them. Hikers come with bright-colored packs and jangling water containers. Chattering, they think they see the forest, and they are satisfied. They gape at the trees, wide and strong with years; they jump at cottonmouths and copperheads. *Watch for snakes*, they say, as if the snakes should not watch for them. Those hikers will kill if cornered. Snakes go about their own business, slither away if given half a chance. They bother nothing and no one.

Some are hunters. They come with guns and knives and silly gadgets; pale-skinned, they dress in green-patched clothes, as if color will hide them from the birds and deer and creeping things. They come to take and kill, and they do not say thank you. I hate them most of all. When their gadgets fail and their guns jam, I laugh from the bushes. Sometimes they look up and search, weak eyes flicking, nervous. I do not worry. They will not see me if I do not want to be seen, and why show myself to greedy people? They will suck dry whatever loves them.

I refuse to be loved.

But I watch the people anyway. They will steal and burn,

maim and kill. They throw their trash in the leaves as if, forgotten, it will disappear. But I will not forget.

There is only one I do not hate. She comes from a battered house on the forest's edge, a house loud with anger and sadness. When the anger and sadness become too much, she slips down a green trail into the forest's wild heart. I watch the others because I must, but I watch her because I like to. She is different from the others. Her long hair falls down her back; her legs are long and good for walking. Her pale skin is creamy instead of reddish. I like her because she does not come to take. She comes to find a place for herself instead. I understand that. The whole forest is my place, but I will share it with her. She does not leave trash or kill what she does not need.

One morning, when the leaves have burst to full green, she stalks under the trees, angry but lonely underneath. Most of the people think they are not lonely, but sadness leaks from this girl like water from a spring. *I will be your friend*, I want to tell her, but I stay hidden. She walks far. She takes the smaller trails, tread by deer and forest creatures, and she does not lose them. I watch her pass under twining trumpet vine, past trees older than the words she knows. The killers come with a plan, and the hikers come with a destination, but this girl has neither. She likes the woods for themselves.

The girl finds a place by a rushing stream. She sits on the cool moss, and she is quiet. Most people are only quiet when they want to kill, and this is another reason I like the girl: she is patient with silence. Woodpeckers thrum; birds sing afternoon songs in the drowsy sunshine. The forest is green and beautiful, honeysuckle scented. The girl dips a toe in the water.

Quickly, she glances around her, as if people might appear in the forest's secret heart, but there is no one. The girl sheds clothes until she stands naked on the moss. She is lovely, all long lines and pale skin, dark hair and dark eyes. Her breasts are small but pretty, with brown-tipped nipples, and the hair between her legs is short and tight curled. It looks soft as fur, and I am seized with a sudden wish to pet her there. She would stretch and purr and sigh even louder than before.

When she turns, she flips her hair to the side, and I see the picture on her back.

It is a palmetto, etched and shaded lovingly. Above it hangs a crescent moon. It must have hurt her—a picture like that would take a long time of sitting still. I like that this girl can sit so still for so long, and she carried a piece of the forest on her back. I would like to carry the forest on my skin, I decide. I would like vines to twine my body and keep me safe.

She does not mind being naked in the forest. She stretches, yawns, then ventures to dip another toe in the water. She seems to make a decision, and I watch as her body disappears into the stream, first her pretty feet, then her pale legs, her round backside. The current breaks around her as she steps the middle of the stream; she drops, and her long, dark hair floats on the current. When she flips on her back, it sinks, and her nipples break the surface, two ripe, brown berries. She wiggles her toes as she stares at the leafy canopy, then closes her eyes.

She stays like that for a long time, floating as the stream babbles around her. I like her silence. Other people come into the forest with bells, with music, and they are afraid. They think their noise will ward away danger. But the girl is neither noisy nor frightened.

I think about this as she floats alone, silent. Her hair sinks. Maybe she should be frightened. Bears and alligators lurk in this forest. So does the black panther no one believes in, not anymore. Is she foolish or brave? Honeysuckle scent hangs languid in the air, like a half-realized thought, and small creatures rustle quietly about their business. The girl is not bold but respectful. She treats the forest as if it was her home. And since it is my home, I am grateful.

Something splashes quietly, and the girl drops her feet, then looks upstream. She stills. In the stream's bend, where it snags into cattails and caught logs, a snowy egret is stalking. It reminds me of the girl, all long legs and pale grace. Vigilant, it eyes the water. The girl and I watch together as it strikes downward, one swift moment of its snake-like neck, then raises its head to swallow a silvery flash of fish. The girl smiles like she has a secret, and the egret gulps, then goes still again.

The girl stays low in the water, only her head visible. The egret does not notice her, and seconds stretch to minutes. The sun-dappled stream sings into our silence. I watch the girl as much as I watch the egret, and I like her more and more. As it steps through the shallows, precise as a dancer, I hope it will strike again, not for the delight of seeing it succeed, but for the curve of the girl's smile. I would like her to smile at me like that.

The egret flies away. The girl stands. Water streams from her back; her hair is a fat, wet rope. It smacks her skin with a wet slap, and she wades from the water. The hair between her legs is slicked down. She is soaked and dripping and beautiful, and when she flicks water from her arms, it flies into flinging droplets. She shucks water from her legs and pulls her underclothes on, grimacing as they stick her to her, then yanks on her top. I wish she would not. I wish she would lie naked and beautiful on the moss, would watch the leaves ruffle in the high up breeze. But she dresses, and I watch her walk away.

I follow. *Stay*, I want to tell her. *I am not done watching you.* It startles me. I do not like people. But this girl's shoes make no sound on the soft leaves. I could be quiet with her. I could show her the forest's secret heart, the woodpeckers and otters, the alligators sunk deep in the mud, and she would smile for me. I would like that, I think. I would like that very much.

When she leaves the forest, walks into the field behind her battered house, I linger. She takes off her shoes on the rotten wood porch, then shakes out her hair again and goes inside.

I have not spoken to anyone in so long. People are loud, and they will hurt you if you give them the chance. But maybe not her. Maybe she would be quiet with me like she is quiet with the forest.

Maybe next time, I will speak to her.

Acknowledgments

As I continued writing Southern Gothic stories set in the tangled swamp country of Lower Congaree, I dreamed of seeing them collected in one place. I'm grateful to all the people who helped make that dream a reality.

Thank you, first of all, to some of the first and best people I remain lucky enough to call ride or die friends: the ones I could still call to bury the proverbial body, who rolled twenty-sided dice with me through Mountain Dew-fueled nights in low ceilinged rooms, and who, most importantly for this particular occasion, agreed on some late nights to climb into my old car floored with soda cans and fast food bags. We'd smoke Parliaments while we drove up Bluff Road, past the stadium and the red dot and under the interstate, past the bail bond places. Then pinewoods would rise around us. The dark would start then, that rural dark barely cut by headlights that never seemed to stretch far enough. We'd cut right as the road split. The swamp started soon after. And oh, it was black back there. We went to the swamp to scare ourselves and my God, we did. I swore I brought something back with me once. Rob, you said I did, too. Joey, you said you felt it outside the window of that apartment on Harden Street.

Joey, Rob and Maren. Miles have passed, and time. Love endures.

I owe a debt of gratitude to the midwives of these stories, the editors who brought them into the world. Editors are the unsung heroes of the writing world. Their names often appear only as tiny print on the inside flaps of magazines; if they're lucky, they score the front cover of an anthology. Editors make books soar, and readers never know how much they owe those quiet people laboring tirelessly in the background. Thank you particularly to the team at *Tales to Terrify*, who brought to life "For Thine is the Kingdom," and the brilliant Cameron Trost, who included "Questions a Man Ought Not to Ask" in *The Black Beacon Book of Horror*. Enormous gratitude as well to Leon Perniciaro and T.J. Price at *Haven Spec*, who accepted "Folded in Light" on the strength of its writing when the ending was a trainwreck. Leon, thank you for your patience and help, without which the story wouldn't be what it is now.

To include enough thanks to D.L., Cyan, and Rebecca at Undertaker Books would take a book in itself. They rescued *Ink Vine* from obscurity, and they did it lightning fast. They're hugely talented and boundlessly kind. D.L. is an amazing editor. Cyan's books are beautiful. I can never, ever repay the kindness and generosity I've found with them, and I'll always be grateful I fell over backward into working with such wonderful people. You put up with me and support me and never fail to like me anyway. I'm so grateful.

Rebecca Cuthbert. You're brilliant and one of the best editors I've ever had the pleasure to work with. *Ink Vine* wouldn't be the novella it is without your tireless effort. You never fail to get what I'm trying to do—and to help me understand how I could do it better. Thank you for your endless support, not just for my last, or this one, but for everything always. Your selflessness and hard work remain a shining example I try my best to follow. I love you to bits.

Joey and Denise. There's no place to begin and no place to end—Babou loathes every houseguest but you two. Take from that what you will. You've both saved my life too many times to count. I love you.

These stories would not exist without my husband, Chris, and my sons. I love you all. You give me space and grace and love and laughter. Thank you, and there I run out of words, because there are none.

About the Author

Elizabeth Broadbent (she/her) is the author of *Ink Vine* (Undertaker Books), *Ninety-Eight Sabers* (Undertaker Books), and *Blood Cypress* (Raw Dog Screaming Press).

Her speculative fiction has appeared with *Hyphenpunk, Tales to Terrify, If There's Anyone Left, Penumbric,* and *The Cafe Irreal,* among other places. During her long career as a journalist, her nonfiction appeared in places such as *The Washington Post, Insider, Time,* and *ADDitude Magazine.* She has appeared on MSNBC, CNN, BBC World News, NPR's *All Things Considered,* and Canadian National Public Radio.

An exile from South Carolina swamp country, she lives in Richmond with her best friend/husband, her three sons, four cats, two dogs, and a flock of crows.

- instagram.com/eabroadbent
- facebook.com/WriterElizabethBroadbent
- tiktok.com/@eabroadbent
- threads.com/@eabroadbent
- bsky.app/profile/elizabethbroadbent.bsky.social
- amazon.com/stores/Elizabeth-Broadbent/author/B0BBBQQ66T

Thank You from Undertaker Books

Thank you for reading Ink Vine and Other Swamp Stories

We appreciate your support of Undertaker Books, as well as all of the indie authors.

Please leave us a review on Goodreads and/or Amazon.

If you are a fan of horror stories and tales, you'll want to follow Undertaker Books.

We're bringing you stories to take to your grave.

www.ingramcontent.com/pod-product-compliance
Lightning Source LLC
LaVergne TN
LVHW040055080526
838202LV00045B/3648